RANGERS UNIVERSE

Slave Traders

DOUGLAS JAMES CHEATHAM

Rangers Universe: Slave Traders

ISBN
978-1-955205-50-4 (Paperback)
978-1-955205-49-8 (eBook)

By Douglas James Cheatham

Cameron Summer's story (Main Rangers plot)

Rangers Universe: Slave Traders
Rangers Universe: Search for Justice
Rangers Universe: Return of the Imperium

Up Next:

Rangers Universe: Betrayal

Find Rangers Universe character list and galaxy map after the book.

RANGERS UNIVERSE DEDICATION

First and foremost, I want to thank my Savior and LORD Jesus Christ for my ability to write and create. This does not make Rangers Universe a Christian book series although I have tried in some regards to do so. This includes a creation-based timeline, and only one God.

Not long ago I made a few mistakes and cast a series of demons into my mind. Crazy right? Well it's true and very real. Someday I pray to have the courage to explain what saw and why I did what I did it.

Thankfully, Jesus saw a better way and pulled my mind out of hell.

ACKNOWLEDGMENTS

I want to give huge thanks and congratulations to my friend and partner Kody Moreno. Thank you, without your assistance I would not have broken the Multiverse barrier.

Thank you, Kindle Direct Publishing. You have made this so easy. From the covers to the overall process. Thank you.

I want to thank my Mother, Ronda Cheatham for her amazing work on the back covers. Thank you for finding the perfect phrasing.

Thanks to my buddy Stinky (Zach Douglass) for all your help with beta-reading! Glad you enjoyed.

I want to thank all editors, proof-readers, beta-readers and Adventure in Known space players. The Rangers Universe would not be the same without you. Thanks again.

CHAPTER LIST

Book Intro: Slave Trader

Year 3242: Line of recorded messages between Infantry Commander Casey Jonas Knight and High Councilman Arland of the Ranger Empire.

Casey Knight

"Fifteen hours ago, the united Draith clans started a new offensive. Saal'li'Mar's fleet broke through our bases on Miikson, Tatith, and Quia. They have also retaken Gaa'nor and Bor'rel. Please advise."

High Councilman Arland

"Where are they going now?"

Casey Knight

"Our line of fortresses. They are planning to hit all at once. From Braxton to De'Voy. Also, inform the Human Republic we are tracking Buul'Vin and No'Vaa's fleets. Their heading for the outer colonies of Agron, Quin and Brighton. We suspect they will cut off the Human's support and hit De'Voy from two sides. My team is on Cantton. We will have an opening in a few hours and can hit them hard. With luck this will turn their fleet around. Please advise."

High Councilman Arland

"Head to Brighton and help the Humans track the movement of their fleet. That is an order, Commander."

Casey Knight

I'll take that under advisement.

INTO THE LION'S DEN

Cameron walked down the dusty streets of Lancing, one of the larger colonies on Agron. She was originally born on the small planet Zail, a trading community with lush farmlands, located on the far reaches of Ranger controlled space. She had always loved the landscape—green rolling hills as far as the eye could see.

Cameron was a Ranger-Telekinetic. In being such, she was feared and scorned by her own people. They said she would lose it and go crazy like the last great Telekinetic, Simon Cail. During the final year of the Accaren war, two hundred years earlier. One fateful night, the famed Battalion Commander lost his mind and killed his entire platoon. Since that day Ranger-Telekinetics had been feared and were banned from becoming a Battalion Commander.

Cameron's second ascension was Ranger-Sense, this allowed her to distinguish an individual's aura, and in time she would be able to also sense their strength.

At the age of eleven, tragedy struck.

Cameron remembered her Grandfather —Hayden walk into her room. He informed the young Ranger that her parents had died in a shuttle accident on their way to Rydon.

After that day, her world, her universe, everything changed. Hayden stepped in and did his best to take over for her parents. To make matters worse, she started having more issues in school. Hayden managed to find a job on Agron. Compared to her home, the planet was a cold and rocky wasteland, however, the Humans were kind and welcoming. Instead of reacting to her in fear, the kids loved, and dreamed of having abilities of their own. Life had become a lot harder. They had just enough money for food, and a small home in the center of the small mining town.

No eccentricities.

The rain always seemed to fall from the heavens, Cameron felt like the sun would never peak out from behind the thick clouds. She continued her walk home from school in silence. From the skies above, she heard a loud buzz. Cameron saw hundreds of Draith controlled drones darted back and forth. They swooped around, targeted what little defense platforms the Human settlement had and left the city open for invasion.

Cameron knew exactly what the ships were and the danger they carried.

Draith, she panicked.

Cameron was terrified and ran to the one place that was safe—home.

She threw open the door and called for her Grandfather, but he was not there. The battle raged around her and Cameron heard the terrifying sound of the Draith invade. Humans screamed and ran past the house and desperately searched for cover. Cameron slammed and locked the door. She sprinted into her room and crawled under the medium sized bed.

Explosions shook the house and ships buzzed overhead.

Cameron's heart nearly stopped as the door burst open and was nearly kicked off its hinges.

Heavy boots sounded and shook the room. From under the bed, Cameron saw the armored boots of a Draith Hunt Master. He stood two and a half meters in height and was muscular but thin. His entire body was covered in silver armor, except for his mouth and sharp teeth. He carried a tri-shot battle rifle and was unable to stand to full height in the Human style home.

Cameron held her breath, closed her eyes and did not move.

Don't see me, gods please don't let them find me, Cameron repeated in her mind and nearly burst into tears at the thought. She had heard stories and knew what terrible fate she would suffer if they found out she was a Ranger. If they thought she was Human, they would most likely take her into slavery.

The thought made her angry, but Cameron knew at her young age she could never fight back with her powerful ascension.

She screamed as the Draith sprinted forward and ripped the bed to the side. He towered over her with menacing silver eyes. They were fixed on her with a hatred she had never witnessed. She pressed her back against the wall and screamed for help. He grabbed her by the hair and drug her kicking out of the house.

"Silence Human," the Hunt Master commanded in a deep voice.

"Let me stand!" she screamed back.

The Draith threw her to the ground and motioned for her to join a group of Humans already captured and being kept in the center of town.

"Move slave," the Draith said to her repulsion.

Cameron glared and moved into the group. She put her hands in the pockets of her jacket and pulled up the hood. The rain beat down and Cameron lost all hope.

She stared around and saw over a dozen Draith Hunters. They had jet black armor with a purple tint. She turned around and looked for her Grandfather but could not find him.

A large ship descended and landed a few hundred meters from her location. It was followed by a second vessel which set down closer. Soon after, they were approached by two Humans.

Cameron focused in and noticed they were different. The one was well dressed in a black suit with matching shoulder length hair. The second was a well build man with short blond hair, a white t-shirt, and blue jeans. He wore black combat boots and a matching leather jacket. His light blue eyes were fixed on the Draith as he guarded the smaller Human.

He's not Human. A Ranger? Cameron thought to herself.

She was confused by this. Rangers were not mercenaries, and they did not sell out to the highest bidder. She could not believe that one of her own people could ever work for such scum as a slaver. Cameron continued to stare at the mysterious Ranger and after a few moments his eyes met with hers.

He leaned forward and whispered a few words into the slave trader's ear. After a moment, the slave trader subtly glanced over at her. He gave a nod of his head and agreed with something the Ranger had said. The man in the black suit made his way over to the Draith Hunt Master and started negotiations. Cameron's eyes darted back to the enigmatic Ranger who made his way over to her.

She wanted to escape, but knew it was impossible.

He knelt so they were at eye level.

"Don't be scared little one," he said in a quiet tone.

Cameron shook as she stood, not sure of what to do.

"What race are you?" he asked.

"I'm like you," she whispered and pointed at his chest.

"Shh…do you know what will happen if they find you?" he quietly replied.

Cameron could not speak the words and nodded fearfully in response.

"Do not use your ascension and stay quiet," he warned.

The Ranger turned and rejoined the slave trader. After a few more minutes, a deal was struck between the Draith and the Human.

The Draith guards surrounded the slaves. With weapons raised, the guards rounded up the Humans and loaded them into the large slave barge.

Cameron walked up the ramp with her head down. She nearly screamed when someone grabbed her by the arm and pulled her to the side. Before she knew what was happening, Cameron was lifted off the ground and set down out of sight from the nearby Hunters.

She quickly looked up and saw the enigmatic Ranger who had spoken to her only minutes before.

"You're riding with us," he said with a smile.

He put his hand on her back and escorted her to a small Human shuttle. Tears rolled down her cheeks as she gave one last look at her home. In that singular moment, she realized how harsh Known-Space was.

* * *

Cameron sat comfortably on one of the neatly kept leather chairs of the Slave Lords personal shuttle. There were three rows of seats which stretched across the luxurious Human transport, with a mini-bar and back room for privacy. Her eyes darted back to the window that overlooked the planet of Camus.

My new home, she thought to herself.

Cameron looked out and saw a desolate wasteland. A brown desert planet. No trees or mountains, pretty much nothing green. It had been ten hours since Alex Sheridan had brought her on board. After coming onto the transport, he introduced himself and answered a few questions. The man who bought her was called James Ferrell and one of the most powerful Slave Lords in all of Known-Space.

Cameron turned her gaze back over to Ferrell, who stood at the entrance to the cockpit. He was in his mid-thirties, average build and a tanned complexion.

He looks so cold, Cameron thought with repulsion, w*hy did he have to take me*?

Her eyes shifted and peered to the right where Alex sat. He rested comfortably in one of the black chairs across the aisle. The Ranger had told her he was the head of Ferrell's security, personal bodyguard and enforcer. Alex was a fifth ascension Energy-Caster. A Ranger who had the ability to create, control and use energy as a weapon. Simply put, his body created this while his mind allowed him to manipulate the fields.

It makes me sick, she thought in contempt.

According to Ranger culture, military officers would become the political face of the Empire and give their entire lives in service. She had always been told they never sold out. Clearly, she was wrong. She turned back to the window and saw a fleet of Tuskeron warships. They were patrolling the space above Camus. Their job was to make sure no unauthorized vessels flew down to the planet below.

They were rectangular and armed to the teeth with a variety of energy-cannons, missile launchers and an assortment of other firepower strategically placed around the warship's hull.

Overall, the Tuskeron hordes had lower level technology. Weaker than the other major races such as the Rangers, Accarens and the Draith. The hybrids made up for this weakness in sheer numbers. For every Ranger ARC-class cruiser constructed, the Tuskerons could build a dozen of their smaller warships for the same amount of resources. This gave them overwhelming numbers across the entire border of the Human Republic and Ninth Faction space.

The shuttle started its final approach downward toward Ferrell's compound. Cameron was in amazement at the size and beauty of her new home. It was a fortress with hundred-meter-high walls that surrounded the perimeter. Dozens of landing platforms extended out beyond the walls. They were circular with turrets and guards stationed around them.

It's like a castle or a prison, she debated in her mind.

Cameron lurched to the side as the vessel's landing struts pressed down onto the metal platform. The hatch to the shuttle opened and Ferrell exited the ship. Her eyes caught movement and Alex casually sat up. He took to his feet and walked over to her. Cameron ignored him and looked out the window.

"Follow me," he said after a moment.

She quickly took to her feet and followed him silently to the door. Upon exiting the ship, Cameron let out a gasp. A dozen rhino-bred Tuskerons lined the narrow walkway across the pad.

"They're so big," she whispered up to Alex.

Up to that point Cameron had only viewed holo-images of the massive aliens and had never seen them in the flesh. The hybrids were half Human, half rhino and stood three meters in height. They weighed over a thousand pounds and were built of sheer muscle.

"Don't be scared, little one. They're here to protect us," Alex said in a calm tone.

She could not help but stare as Alex led her past the motionless guards. After a few seconds, she made eye contact with one of the behemoths. The black-eyed creature scowled and grunted, causing Cameron to jump back. Alex gave out a slight chuckle at her reaction and led her into the fortress.

She was escorted through the beautiful and eloquent hallways. Silk drapes were on every window. Portraits, statues and other forms of artwork decorated the promenade. They were passed by three young women. Each scantily clad, wearing nothing more than a bikini top and a long white skirt.

"They're slaves," Alex said and answered her question before it could be asked.

"They're allowed to walk around freely?" Cameron replied with confusion.

Her thirteen-year-old mind was unaccustomed to the details of slavery or how the process worked.

"Yes. You'll find that there is a great deal of variety here. Many of the slaves are happy and live very comfortable lives," Alex replied.

This was hard for Cameron to accept, but she was not going to argue with one of the few bright sides she had seen so far. They made their way to a great set of doors. They stood four-and-a-half meters tall and was guarded by two Tuskerons. The hybrids assault-rifles were slung over their backs. The weapons were not only taller than her but were double Cameron's bodyweight.

Alex motioned with his hand, and the two guards opened the doors. They swung inward and Cameron's jaw dropped as Alex led her into Ferrell's throne room.

There were long purple tapestries that stretched down from the nine-meter ceiling. Numerous life size statues of Ferrell, his father and the rest of his bloodline were symmetrically placed on both sides of the path. On the other side of the throne room, Ferrell sat motionless on a red tinted wooden throne. The chair was ornate yet not overly extravagant and was simplistic in its design. The chair was raised off the ground by a hexagon platform with over a dozen sets of stairs.

Cameron felt Alex's strong hand press firmly against the center of her back and guide Cameron forward to the base of the hexagon. She gazed up the stairs that led to Ferrell's throne.

Ferrell stayed silent. He sat there in deep contemplation. His legs were crossed with his hand stroking his chin. Alex nudged her forward, and Cameron lowered her head in fear.

"What is your name?" the Slave Lord asked in a baritone voice.

"Cameron," she quivered.

"What is your full name, Cameron?" he clarified.

She looked back to Alex who gave a nod of his head, signifying her to answer.

"Cameron Lynn Summers," she responded after a moment.

"And what race are you?" he pressed and moved to the edge of his seat.

She did not answer and kept her hands neatly clasped behind her back. The Slave Lord held his gaze with his piercing brown eyes fixed on the young Ranger.

"I already know you're a Ranger. Why? Because I have seen that same look of pride and the unfounded arrogance that accompanies it. Do you know what the common denominator is?" he queried.

Ferrell stood up, walked down the stairs and stopped less than a meter from her.

"I have seen these two traits before in every Ranger I've encountered. Even my own bodyguard, who I have come to trust and respect. He still has that same smug, conceited smirk. So, it is clear you're a Ranger, but what's your ascension?" he hissed condescendingly.

"I can feel the differences between auras, sir," she replied and told half the truth.

"Is that so?" he sneered

"I can tell you're a Human, Alex is a Ranger, and that there are two Tuskerons behind that door," Cameron replied and pointed to the entrance.

"Sense is a secondary ability, Cameron. What's your primary ascension?" Alex interjected.

"That is my primary skill," she lied.

Ferrell shook his head, walked up the hexagon and retook his seat upon the throne.

"Take her to the dungeons. We'll see if that makes her more cooperative," he commanded.

Alex grabbed hold of her arm and forcefully led her around the throne.

"Don't worry, James. I'll talk some sense into her," the Energy-Caster replied as he passed the slaver.

Sure, you will, she thought with disbelief.

On the other side of the throne was a walkway. It spanned a half-dozen meters and had doors on either side. They stopped at the first door to the left. It opened, and they boarded a small powerlift. After a moment, the doors shut and sealed tightly.

"Sub-level one," Alex said to the computer.

Immediately after his command the powerlift started a rapid descent. Her ears popped as they went deeper into the planet.

"There are five levels overall. Each one has their own purpose," Alex explained.

"What are you going to do to me?" she asked fearfully.

"What am I going to do? Nothing. I'm giving you a tour of your new home," he replied, obviously amused by her question.

"This isn't my home," Cameron argued.

"Well, you can keep telling yourself that, Cameron, but it doesn't make it true," he replied calmly.

"Did they take you away from your home by force, or did you start working for Ferrell of your own free will?" she asked bluntly and gazed up at Alex.

She could tell the question caught him a bit off guard.

"That's tricky to answer, so yes and no," he replied in a vague tone.

The powerlift finally reached its destination. The doors opened, and Alex exited the elevator.

"What's that supposed to mean?" Cameron asked.

"I know about accountability firsthand. I have seen the true face of our people. The overwhelming amounts of corruption. The lies that were told over and over. Not to mention the countless lives the Ranger High Council has sacrificed at a whim," he replied in a powerful voice.

She lowered her head in fear. Cameron felt she had asked too many questions or had gone too far. Alex noticed her distress and put his hand under her chin. After a moment, Cameron's eyes lifted and met his kind gaze. A single tear rolled down her tanned cheek, but Alex took his other hand and wiped it from her face.

"You don't need to fear me, little one. But to survive, you'll need to toughen up," he said and tried to calm her.

Cameron stared back into his light blue eyes with an emotionless response.

"Better," he said with a smile.

Alex turned and walked over to a nearby railing that spanned the length of the cavern. The dungeon was carved out of solid rock. It had a high roof with a metal walkway on either side. In the center was a pit. There were rows of holding cells around the border with hundreds of Human and Accaren slaves occupying them.

Cameron stood in shock at the sight before her eyes.

"There are so many," she exclaimed.

"Welcome to the lion's den. This is how James Ferrell rose to the top. He always has plenty of stock to sell off," he said and used the crude slaver's term.

She was appalled by his words and glared up with defiance.

"That's disgusting!" Cameron replied.

Alex merely shrugged at the statement.

"I'm not going to argue with you, Cameron, but this is the world we live in," he said in a firm tone.

"But—"

"No buts. You are the same as every one of those poor bastards down there. You are owned by Ferrell and don't have the luxury of making your own choices," he interrupted.

Cameron remained silent and glared out at the multiplicity of slaves.

I hate you, she thought to herself, *you ripped me away from my home, from my friends, my family and now you have the audacity to tell me I'm property?* Her mind was filled with hatred and overwhelming anger. *I'm a Telekinetic…If I wanted, I could effortlessly throw you off this bridge and crush you in front of the slaves below.*

"Cameron, what is your primary ascension?" Alex asked and ripped her mind back to the present.

Her mind was already made up.

I can't tell them. I can NEVER tell them! she shouted in her mind.

"If I don't get the answers to these questions, I promise you, Ferrell will," he continued in a threatening yet empathetic tone.

"No! I will never tell you!" Cameron screamed at the top of her lungs.

Her eyes caught side of the Tuskeron guards who immediately raised their assault-rifles and aimed them in her direction. Alex stood calmly and raised his hand alerting the guards everything was under control. He took a knee and brought himself to her eye level.

"Please tell me why this is such a big secret, Cameron. Rangers share their abilities, it's common knowledge," he said with confusion, "it's part of our title and pride of being the race we are. I am former Captain Alex Sheridan, fifth ascension Energy-Caster, and you are?

Everything in her wanted to answer. It was polite and what her parents had taught her to do. It was who she was, and Alex knew it.

"Cameron Summers, first ascension Sense-Ranger," she replied and deepened her defiance.

"Why?" Alex replied and did not understand her deception.

"You'll use me," she hissed with purest honesty, "I will never serve you and I will never be a slave!"

A look a clarity swept over his face at her conviction and strength.

"Now that we are finally being honest, Cameron. What is your primary ascension?"

Cameron crossed her arms and bit her lip in response.

"If that's the way you want it. So be it," Alex stood back up and motioned two of the Tuskeron guards over.

"Take her back to the entrance of the throne room," Alex commanded.

The guards approached and took Cameron by the arm. She gave one final glance over to Alex who was in deep thought as he leaned over the edge of the railing. The guards escorted her to the second powerlift that led outside the throne room. Cameron was taken to the door and forced to wait there for what seemed like hours. As she stood, Cameron could hear raised voices coming from inside the throne room.

"Do you really want to bite down on this bullet, James?" she heard Alex say through the door.

"Don't try and lie to me, Sheridan," Ferrell yelled back, "you despise and loathe the Rangers as much as I do. Why is this child so different from the Rangers you've killed over the years?"

She desperately wanted to hear the rest, but their voices dropped to a level that could not be heard through the massive door. Cameron's heart jumped into her throat at the sound of a bell ringing from inside the throne room. The guards opened the door and escorted her to the base of the throne. One of the guards stood a few meters behind her, while the second returned to the door. Just like before, the Slave Lord was fixated on her with a cold, dead stare.

She looked for Alex. He stood to the right in a stoic pose at the top of the stairs. His hands were clasped behind him. His stance and posture made her feel uneasy. His eyes seemed cold and void of emotion.

"Cameron," Ferrell's deep voice growled.

Her head turned and gazed into the brown, almost black irises of her captor.

"I'm going to ask you one more time, what is your primary ascension?"

Why is this so important? she asked herself, but Cameron already knew the answer to her question.

It was control.

"Sense, sir," she said and repeated the same preposterous lie.

Ferrell bit his lip at receiving the same answer.

"As a standard process, I run blood tests on all the slaves that come into my possession. Do you want to know what I found?" he asked with a smirk.

Oh no! Cameron's mind panicked, but she did not let them see it.

Ferrell gave a slight motion of his hand, and a Tuskeron dragged Hayden into the throne room. Her heart swelled at the sight. He had been savagely beaten with blood still dripping from his mouth and nose. This was her worst fear and the Slave Lord had found it. She screamed at the top of her lungs, but the second Tuskeron guard held her in place with its three-fingered hand.

"He's your Grandfather, correct? From your father's side?" Ferrell mocked.

She could hear the sick and twisted pleasure in his voice brought forth by his actions. Her Grandfather tried to stand, but the guard kicked him back to the floor. Her eyes were clouded with tears and her mind consumed with fury. Cameron whipped back and faced the Slave Lord.

"I'll…" she hissed and did not complete the sentence.

"You'll what?" Ferrell growled back and motioned for the Tuskeron to release her.

"I'll grind your bones into the ground! Then I'll…then I'll throw your broken corpse through your self-righteous throne!" she yelled in hatred.

Her normally sweet brown eyes had vanished, and a darker scowl filled her expression.

"I've broken and enslaved far more powerful aliens then you. A stupid, conceited, Ranger bitch. So, do not think for a moment you intimidate me, girl. Let alone frighten me," his voice boomed.

The ground shook as Cameron's rage grew. She raised her left arm and lifted the thousand-pound Tuskeron behind her. Both Ferrell and Alex were caught by surprise. Neither had ever seen a Ranger-Telekinetic before, and in the end never would have made the correct guess to her ascension. Before either could react, Cameron threw the massive animal through the double doors and took out the other guards.

Her attention turned back to Ferrell who watched her in awe. He seemed pleased by what he saw. The anger, wrath, and sheer power of her ability. Cameron reached back and picked up the second Tuskeron who stood next to her Grandfather. With one seamless motion she hurled the beast directly at the Slave Lord. Ferrell ducked down as a blue shield surrounded him. The hybrid bounced off the energy barrier with such force it flew within a few meters of the ceiling and crashed through the back wall of the throne room.

Inside the bubble, Ferrell was on his hands and knees. He had a look of fear, backed up by anger. She knew a Human could not create an energy field. Her eyes turned to Alex who had his right arm extended, maintaining the protective barrier around Ferrell. Using her right hand, Cameron grabbed a hold of the Energy-Caster, lifted him up, and slammed his body against the hexagon.

Her attention turned back to her Grandfather, who struggled to crawl. Her gaze caught sight of the final Tuskeron who had recovered at the door. The beast was infuriated by her actions and charged forward. The hybrid's sharpened horn poised to gore her.

A split second before contact, a blue shield erupted between them. The Tuskeron was stopped dead in his tracks by the solid wall of energy. It stumbled around and then collapsed to the ground with a thud.

"Stand down, Cameron," a voice said behind her.

She whipped around and saw Alex standing back on the stairs. He seemed a little shook up while blood ran down his face from a deep cut.

"Traitor!" Cameron screamed in reply, "you're not a slave, you do this of your own free will!"

"You're right, and I have my own reasons for doing so. Now stand down, or I'll put you down," he threatened.

She lifted her arm but before she could take hold, a heavy object impacted against her chest. Cameron lost her balance and fell to the ground. Alex had launched a concentrated energy burst.

"That's a warning shot!" he yelled over.

He took a step down the stairs, blue energy swirled around his clenched fists while his gaze stayed fixed on her. Cameron struggled to her feet.

"Don't do it!" he warned.

She did not listen.

Cameron raised her arm and was hit by a second energy burst that contacted her jaw. Her long brown hair whipped to the side and Cameron fell to the ground out cold.

*   *   *

Her eyes opened slowly. Cameron found herself in a small, dark prison cell. Her jaw was stiff, and she had a pounding headache. She put her hands over her face to cover up the horrible, putrid smell of the dungeon.

As the minutes ticked by her situation started to sink in. She was alone in a dark, miserable place. Her heart jumped into her throat as she played future scenarios in her mind. Her thoughts turned to her Grandfather.

"What have I done? I sentenced him to death! Why do you hate me?" Cameron screamed out to the cell roof and imagined the brilliant blue skies above.

Her parents had indoctrinated her with the Ranger's core beliefs. Cameron questioned why she followed the teachings of the gods who allowed her parents to be killed. She struggled to her feet, brushed off her pants, and walked up to the orange tinted barrier. Cameron touched her finger to the shield but was instantly shocked and pulled her hand back.

"Ouch!" she exclaimed.

She rubbed the feeling back into her fingers and forearm, which had become numb.

"Careful, these shields were designed to withstand an inferno from a fifth ascension Fire-Caster," a familiar voice sounded.

Alex walked out of the shadows and stood on the other side of the cell.

Cameron stayed silent, crossed her arms and took a seat on the far side of her cell.

"Are you hungry?" Alex asked in a compassionate tone.

"I'm not hungry," she replied, but it was a lie. Cameron was starving, "why do you care?"

Alex bent down to his haunches and rested his hands on his legs.

"In the throne room you could have chosen to surrender, to give in, but you surprised us all. You not only held your ground against overwhelming numbers, but more importantly you fought to your last breath. That merit alone deserves recognition," he said with pride.

Cameron felt cold. She pulled her knees up to her chest as she thought about his statement.

"Why should I care what you think of me? You murdered my Grandpa and I'll be locked in this horrible place forever," she spouted back.

Alex lowered his head and took a deep breath before responding.

"I can't blame you for feeling that way, but you're wrong."

Cameron was surprised by his words and frustrated by his cryptic answer.

"What is that supposed to mean?" she snapped.

"Hayden is alive."

Her heart swelled with joy at the news. She quickly made it to her feet and rushed over to the shield.

"Can I see him?" she pleaded.

"Well, that's going to depend on this chat were having," Alex replied.

Cameron shoved her hands in her pockets and stared at the stone floor.

"Let me ask you a question, Cameron, where were you born?" he asked.

"Zail," she replied.

"So, you were born on a Ranger controlled planet. How did our people react to your ascension?" he questioned.

"They hated me. They said I would become Simon Cail," she replied in honest fashion.

"Do you think that's right? Do you want to be loyal to a race that hates and despises you?" Alex asked.

She knew what Alex was getting at and what he wanted.

"You have a choice to make. Option one, bow before Ferrell, be branded and serve him. I promise to protect you, Cameron. You will still be a slave. But, compared to most of the poor souls who ended up in this place, you will live a very comfortable life," he stated.

She thought about the offer for a moment. She had heard and seen the nano-brands of slavers in the past. It was something that feared the young Ranger. Deep down, Cameron knew once the nanites touched her olive skin she would never be the same. She would always be branded and recognized as a slave.

"And before you ask, you don't want to know the second option," he continued in a stern tone.

Although her choices were grim, there was one clear answer.

"I will," she said under her breath.

"I'm sorry, what was that?" Alex replied and asked for clarification.

"I will serve him," Cameron said again and tried to hold back her tears, "I will bow and be branded as a slave."

Alex stood up and lowered the energy shield. He extended his hand and motioned for her to exit the disgusting cell. Cameron stepped out into the dark hallway. It looked like an endless abyss. Rows and rows of shielded cells which stretched beyond her vision.

"Where are we?" she asked softly as they started making the journey back to the powerlift.

"This is the fourth level of the dungeon. The first two levels which you saw earlier are for common slaves, basic races such as Humans and Accarens. Levels three and four are reserved for the more colorful aliens," he explained.

"But you said earlier there were five levels?" she questioned.

"Good on you for remembering that. The fifth level was specifically designed to hold the most dangerous beings Ferrell has ever encountered. The level itself is locked down and can only be accessed by a chosen few," he replied with a smile.

His words piqued her curiosity.

"What's down there?" she asked.

Alex smiled, he stopped and knelt in front of her.

"Have you ever heard of the Xan?" he questioned.

Cameron shook her head in response, out of all the races in Known-Space. The Xan were a race she had never heard mentioned or referenced.

"That's good. I hope you never have to," Alex replied cryptically.

She was a bit confused by his answer but decided not to press the issue. Upon reaching the powerlift, Cameron gave one final look down the endless hallway. In that moment she felt the aura of a powerful alien. Cameron put her hands over her ears as she heard the muffled voice of the creature.

"You can feel them, can't you?" Alex asked.

"Yes," she replied almost out of breath. "I can hear their thoughts."

"Come on, we need to get you out of here," Alex said, and put his hand on her back.

He guided her onto the powerlift and started their ascent to the main level. Cameron put her hands back in her pockets and stared down at the grey floor.

"Don't be nervous," he said in a calming tone, "I'll be there the whole time."

Cameron opened her eyes and shifted her gaze to him. Before she could respond, the powerlift stopped and the door opened. They walked out and made their way around the hexagon shaped staircase. Cameron observed the Slave Lord. He was perched comfortably on the ornate throne. Ferrell was dressed in black and blended perfectly with the reddish chair. His hands rested comfortably on his knees.

"What is your name and race?" he sneered in a deep, menacing voice.

"Cameron Lynn Summers, first ascension Telekinetic and Sense-Ranger," she replied and used proper grammar for her ascension.

"Do you swear to follow my orders, my commands?" Ferrell questioned.

"Yes, sir," she replied without hesitation.

Surprised by her quick response, Ferrell took to his feet, walked down the stairs and towered over her.

"Do you swear to protect me, to kill or do any other action I require?"

Cameron struggled and fought to say the words.

"Yes, sir," she finally spit out.

"Good. Now bow before your master," he commanded in a sinister tone.

Cameron closed her eyes to control her overwhelming emotions, but it was no use. Tears rolled down her face uncontrollably as she fell to her knees and bowed before the Slave Lord. Ferrell turned around and remade the short journey to his wooden throne. He sat comfortably and kept his piercing gaze on the sobbing Ranger.

"Alex, it's time," Ferrell commanded and motioned to his enforcer.

Alex stepped forward. Cameron's eyes opened wide as he pulled out a nanite-brand. It was circular and fit in his hand. When activated, the device injected the being with nanites. These microscopic robots formed into a programmed symbol. This cut into the skin and left a permanent scar.

Culturally it meant more. Cameron knew once it touched her skin, she would never be the same. A commitment to her being a slave. By Ninth Faction and Accaren law she would legally belong to Ferrell. She hated the thought, but this was the choice being forced upon her.

Alex knelt next to her, pulled out a leather strap and handed it to her.

"Bite down," he said in a quiet voice, "it will make it easier."

Cameron nodded her understanding. She took the leather strap and pressed it firmly between her teeth.

"Lift up the back of your shirt," Alex ordered.

Cameron gently pulled up the back of her shirt and held it at the base of her neck. Cameron stayed on her knees and held the lower front of her shirt in place with her elbows.

The device made a high pitch whine as it powered up. Her heart pounded while her breaths became rapid. Cameron felt Alex's strong hand grip her shoulder. A sharp pinch echoed through her body as the injector pierced the skin. A second later she felt a searing pain as the nanites carved Ferrell's mark in her shoulder. This was unlike anything she had felt before.

Cameron tried to bite down but could not stand the pain. She screamed out in agony and let the strap fall from her mouth. She gasped for air as tears rolled uncontrollably down her cheeks.

Her worst fears had happened. She had not only been branded but Cameron had willingly given herself to Ferrell. She could not rise and cried out in pain.

"Take her to her quarters," Ferrell commanded.

Alex pulled down her shirt and helped Cameron to her feet. She gasped as the material shirt rubbed against the tender skin. Alex led the way and the pair exited the throne room.

BREAKOUT

Night had fallen over Ferrell's compound. It had only been fifteen minutes since Cameron had thrown away her morality and knelt before the Slave Lord. Her shoulder ached and she knew it would be sometime before the brand would heal. She felt dirty and still a bit queasy after the encounter. The teen Ranger was exhausted and had barely gotten any sleep in the past thirty hours.

Alex was a few steps ahead of her and led the way to her new quarters. Cameron had seen a few rooms in passing and was not impressed. They were small with two or three bunkbeds that stretched up to the ceiling and appeared to house six slaves.

At least I'll have a bed, Cameron thought pessimistically.

After a few minutes, they came to a wooden door with a silver handle. Alex opened it and walked into the pitch-black room. Cameron peered in but could not make out any distinguishing features.

Alex clapped his hands and the lights turned on. Her jaw dropped at the sight. The room was stunning and spacious. There was a large bed in the center with curtains around the edges. Cameron took a few steps deeper into the room, amazed by what she saw.

"So, what do you think?" Alex asked with a smile.

"Alex…It's so beautiful," she remarked.

"I'm glad you like it. Let me give you a tour," he replied.

They walked forward and stopped at a full-size armoire. He motioned for her to open the closet. As Cameron did, she let out a slight gasp. There were multiple shelves of shorts, with a few sets of pants. Hanging above, were over a dozen tank-tops, cap and long sleeve shirts. They were mixed in color but mostly purple and white. They were similar style to the clothing she wore, just higher quality. Cameron touched and ran her small fingers over the thick cotton material.

"They're so soft," she exclaimed with a smile.

Alex chuckled as he watched her excitement unfold. To the left of the tank-tops were two cold weather jackets, a brown leather blazer with what appeared to be a black shroud with a silver lining.

"Pretty," she mumbled under her breath.

Her eyes shifted to the bottom of the armoire, where she saw six pairs of ankle-high boots neatly placed on the bottom shelf. Cameron closed the closet door and followed Alex into the bathroom. There was a large sink, with water continuously flowing over the bronze fixture. The floor was tile with a walk-in shower to the left.

They walked out of the bathroom, around the bed and out onto the balcony which stretched across the length of the room. Cameron made her way to the railing and gazed out. The moon shown down, illuminating the other buildings and slave bazaar below.

"I don't understand. I didn't think slaves had any possessions," she stated with confusion.

Alex merely laughed at her simplistic view of the world.

"Well, you have to remember, Cameron, there are different types of slaves. Each one has their own purpose, freedoms and value to go with it," he explained.

Cameron was not sure what Alex meant and turned her gaze back to the bazaar.

"Don't worry, I'll explain the differences tomorrow, but for tonight let's talk about your role."

Her heart jumped into her chest. Cameron felt unsure if she wanted to hear what Alex had to tell her, but there was no point in running away. She had seen firsthand where that led.

"You're special, even more than me. You will be trained as a bodyguard and in time will take my place as Ferrell's enforcer."

"Why does Ferrell need so many Rangers to guard him?" Cameron questioned.

"For a number of reasons. First off, Ferrell is a Slave Lord. Do you know what that means?" he asked.

Cameron shook her head in response.

"At any given point there could be up to twelve Slave Lords spread over Ninth Faction and Accaren space. Each one battling for power. For the past ten years Ferrell has kept his seat at the top," Alex explained and turned his gaze out to the compound.

"Seems peaceful, doesn't it?" he asked.

"Yes," she replied.

"Well, that could change in a heartbeat. You and I might have to chase down a runaway slave. We could come under attack from another Slave Lord, Ranger or whatever else might come here. The point is there is always something happening on Camus," he said with a smile.

Alex turned and motioned for them to go back inside. Cameron walked over and took a seat on the edge of the cushy bed. Alex followed and knelt in front of her.

"So, that's why I'm here? To protect a Slave Lord?" Cameron asked.

"That will be one of your duties, yes. You will also help with raids, slave transport and a variety of other items. Rule number one and single handedly the most important. No one can know you're a Telekinetic," he replied and finished with the warning.

"So, I can't use my abilities?" Cameron questioned.

"Oh, you can, and you will. There just can't be any witnesses. That's why you have the shroud, it will conceal your identity when we're on a raid," Alex corrected.

"What if someone finds out?" Cameron asked tentatively.

"I'll kill them. If anyone knew Ferrell had a Ranger-Telekinetic... It would be war, not just with the other Slave Lords. The Rangers, Humans and every other race would target us," Alex replied in a dark tone.

Cameron lowered her head. Her exhausted mind desperately tried to absorb the information. He put his hand under her chin and lifted her gaze.

"You tired, little one?" he asked in a kind voice.

Cameron nodded her head, barely able to keep her eyes open.

"Get some rest," he said and took to his feet.

Alex walked over to the door, he stopped and turned back to her.

"Do you go by anything other than Cameron? Any form of nickname?" he asked.

"No," she replied.

"Don't worry I'll think of something. Goodnight, Cameron," he said with a grin.

"Goodnight, Alex," Cameron whispered as he shut the door.

She lay motionless. She wanted to make sure she was alone. Cameron carefully tossed back the blankets, sat up and made her way into the bathroom. She stared into the mirror and carefully lifted the back of her shirt.

Cameron saw a deep circular burn on her right shoulder. In the center of the circle was a capital F with three planets above it. They were connected by lines to the circular edge. It was more intricate than she had expected, but Cameron hated it all the same.

She lowered her tank top and made her way back into the bedroom. Cameron carefully laid down and rested her head on the soft pillow. Seconds later, she drifted off into a deep dreamless sleep.

* * *

"Rise and shine!" Alex's voice sounded loudly through the wooden door.

Cameron quickly jumped out of her warm bed. She swiftly ran over to her armoire and put on a pair of shorts, tank-top and boots. Cameron opened the door to see Alex casually leaned against the adjacent wall. He was wearing blue jeans, combat boots, and a white skin-tight t-shirt.

"I'm ready," she muttered, still half asleep.

"Come on kid, we have a lot of ground to cover," he laughed.

Cameron shut the door and followed Alex down the hallway. They made their way to a powerlift. The pair entered and took it down to the base floor. They exited the lift and walked out into the slave bazaar. The morning sun shone down brightly and felt like heaven against her skin. The peaceful marketplace had transformed. There were hundreds of shops along the promenade with scores of Humans and other aliens around them.

"Welcome to the slave bazaar. During the day, the bazaar is open for commerce. Slave traders from around Known-Space come here to buy and sell what stock they have," Alex explained.

They started making their way through the marketplace. Cameron looked around at the wide variety before her eyes. Each shop specialized in a different market. Most of the slaves appeared to be Human but she also saw Accaren, Turkcanon and Tuskeron as well.

They stopped in front of one of the larger shops. The merchant drug a young woman on to the stage and presented her to the crowd. Her hands were bound with a thick rope, and her eyes filled with terror. The shop keeper gave a description of the slave and opened the bidding to the howling mob. Cameron felt sick to her stomach at the sight and ran from Alex's side.

"Cameron!" he yelled after her, but she did not listen.

Cameron ran to the edge of the street and started throwing up in a large flowerpot. A few seconds later, Alex walked up behind her. He knelt and put his strong hand on her back.

"Are you alright?" he asked with concern.

"No. How can you stand it?" she coughed.

"Time," Alex said in a somber tone.

"Who is she?" Cameron questioned.

"She's a parafek," Alex replied.

Alex noticed her lack of understanding and stayed at her level.

"Let me explain. There's a variety of different types of slaves you'll run into. Each one has their own value and can be rated differently. Take Humans versus Accarens for example. Accaren slaves are generally three times the price. Not just because they're stronger, but Accarens are harder to break and control.

"So, what is a parafek?" she asked.

"Parafek is the Accaren word for a sex slave."

Her eyes darted back to the woman as everything became clear. A tear rolled down her cheek as she watched the slaver lead the battered woman off the stage and passed the rope to her new master. Cameron bit her lip in anger.

"I—"

"Alex Sheridan!" a nasally voice sounded behind them.

"Gods…" Alex muttered to himself.

He took to his feet and turned around to face the black-haired stranger. The man was short and had a thin almost scrawny build. He seemed young and could not have been more than nineteen years old. He had four well-built bodyguards around him with a massive alien in the center. She had grey skin with long black hair. The alien had a pencil thin build and stood as tall as a Draith. Her hands were bound with two lead ropes in the guard's hands.

"Conrad Masters. What Draith shit pile did you crawl out of this time?" Alex replied in an annoyed tone.

"Funny, Ranger. I've actually been out building an empire," Conrad replied with pride in his voice.

"What? Did your daddy kick you out?" Alex taunted with a smirk.

"Screw you, Sheridan, screw you. I have my fortune standing behind me, ever seen an A'lur'in warrior before?" Conrad pointed to the tall grey skinned alien.

"I was going to comment. If you think you can control an A'lur'in, you're stupid even for a Human. I'm amazed she hasn't broken loose and killed you already," Alex replied with a laugh and was clearly amused by the thought of Conrad's death.

"No one has seen an A'lur'in in a long time, this is my ticket to wealth and true power," Conrad retorted.

The slaver then turned his gaze to Cameron and walked over. A chill went up her spine as he ogled her from head to toe.

"So, this is what brings you to the bazaar. I approve of Ferrell's good taste," Conrad said with a smirk and slapped Cameron firmly on the behind.

Before she knew what was happening, Alex stepped between them. He put his strong hand around the slavers neck and effortlessly lifted the Human off the ground with his left hand.

"Never touch her again!" Alex yelled, enraged by the slaver's brazen actions.

"And if I do?" Conrad coughed.

"I'll hang your broken corpse outside the front gate to show all visitors the endless stupidity of Conrad Masters, you sick bastard," Alex threatened with a deep growl.

Simultaneously, all four of his bodyguards reached for their weapons. Alex looked over at the guards and back to Conrad.

"Really? Tell your guards to stand down, before I level all of you," Alex sneered.

"Stand down," Conrad coughed.

Alex released the slaver and Conrad fell to the ground. With the guards distracted, the A'lur'in warrior took advantage of the situation. The alien threw her arms from side to side and launched two of the guards into the promenade. The A'lur'in broke free of her restrains and leveled the remaining bodyguards. Alex lifted his arm and threw an energy burst at the A'lur'in, but the alien's reflexes kicked in and allowed her to evade the projectile.

She whipped around, kicked Alex in the chest and threw him to the dirt. The alien hit him with such force, Alex was thrown back a few meters. The A'lur'in made a break for it and took off down the crowded parkway. Within seconds, Alex was back on his feet mobile comm-unit in hand.

"Lock down the compound! We have a female A'lur'in on the loose in the bazaar," Alex yelled. Immediately after his statement, alarms began to sound.

"Come on, Cameron!" Alex yelled back at her and took after the alien.

Cameron followed as fast as her little legs could carry her, but the gap between them grew.

"Keep up, kid!" Alex yelled back.

The warrior darted left and made her way into the back alleyway. Alex followed and soon after both the Energy-Caster and the A'lur'in were out of sight. Cameron whipped around the corner in search of her objective but did not see either of them. She stopped to catch her breath. As she gasped for air, Cameron heard a battle rage in the distance. She took off dead sprint and quickly moved toward the commotion. Upon rounding the final corner Cameron saw Alex. He was engaged in combat with the warrior.

Alex launched two energy bolts. The female alien dodged the assault and closed the gap between them. The A'lur'in lunged forward, but Alex activated his second ability and a massive shockwave burst out from his body. It caught the alien by surprise and threw her against the sandstone building behind her. Alex followed up the defensive maneuver with an energy burst which dropped the alien to her knees.

Alex rushed forward to subdue the alien, but it was a trap. She threw a gut punch and landed an elbow across his face. Alex fell to his hands and knees, winded by the attack. The alien cocked back her arm and swung downward.

Cameron's reflexes kicked in. She reached out with her mind and lifted the alien. Alex rolled back to his feet and threw an energy burst into the A'lur'in's face.

The alien's head snapped back as a sharp crack sounded. Cameron released her grip on the alien. The A'lur'in's lifeless body fell to the ground with a thud. Alex turned to face Cameron. He was a bit wobbly and bruised from his encounter.

"Nice move, kid," he said with a smile.

Out of the corner of Cameron's eye she saw a silhouette in the shadows. She whipped to the side and saw a Human slave girl no more than sixteen. She held a ceramic bowl filled with water and was speechless at the events witnessed. Alex followed Cameron's gaze. A look of dismay filled his expressions upon seeing the slave.

"Son of a bitch," he said under his breath.

The slave girl was terrified and shook.

"I'm sorry—" the slave started.

"What did you see?" Alex's voice boomed.

The woman looked at Cameron, then back to Alex.

"I promise… I promise I won't tell anyone," she desperately pleaded.

"I'm sorry. Wrong place, wrong time," he said in a mournful tone.

Alex cocked back his arm and powered up a massive amount of energy. It formed from his elbow and stretched down to his hand. He threw his arm forward and fired the weapon. It was his fifth ascension and was referred to as the energy-hammer. This was the single greatest weapon Alex had at his disposal.

The energy-hammer shattered the ceramic container and slammed into the girl's chest. The powerful burst lifted the woman off the ground and into the building behind her. A horrible crack sounded as all the bones in her chest and back broke on impact. She slumped to the ground and was killed instantly.

Cameron was speechless, and had no words, curses, or any form of profanity to describe what she had witnessed. She stood motionless, jaw-dropped, with her gaze fixated on the slave girl's lifeless eyes.

"Cameron," she heard Alex say, but she didn't acknowledge him, "Cameron!"

She turned and saw Alex kneel next to her.

"Why—"

"What did I tell you last night?" he interrupted.

Cameron did not respond and kept her hands in her pockets.

"Cameron focus," he continued in a firmer tone.

"You said no one could see me use my ascension. But you—" she stammered.

"Yes! Yes, I did! Because she is only Human. I tried to explain the values of different slaves. That woman is worth nothing compared to you. She was just in the wrong place at the wrong time," he said and cut her off once again.

"I don't want to be special," Cameron cried out as tears rolled down her cheeks.

"I know, but that's not who you are," he replied empathetically.

From behind them, six Tuskerons moved in on their location, weapons raised. Alex took to his feet and approached the lead hybrid.

"Clean this mess up and tell Conrad to take better care of his slaves," he ordered.

"Understood," the Tuskeron replied in a deep voice.

A beep sounded, and Alex pulled out his comm-unit.

"Yes?" he said into the small device.

"I need you in the tactical center ASAP," Ferrell's voice sounded over the comm.

"On our way," Alex replied and hooked the comm back to his belt.

"Come on, little one. We have work to do," he said.

Cameron regained her composure and followed him out of the alleyway. They made their way back into the fortress and up to the throne room. They walked around the reddish chair and down the hallway. The pair made their way to the end and stopped at the last door. Alex entered the code and the door slid open. Cameron followed him at a brisk pace into the tactical center.

The room was large, with Tuskerons monitoring sensors, weapons, fleet movements and other systems. These vital machines gave the hybrids a systems wide view of Camus and other planets in the Ninth Faction. In the center was a raised hexagon platform with a metal railing around it.

Alex and Cameron walked up the small set of stairs and approached Ferrell. The Slave Lord was intensely focused on the terminal in front of him.

"What's the status on the second slave barge?" Ferrell snapped impatiently.

"It just left Vau'Tir, still three hours out," one of the Tuskerons said.

"Unacceptable! Get it done faster!" Ferrell yelled back.

The Slave Lord turned his attention to Alex.

"I heard there was an A'lur'in loose in the bazaar?"

"Blame Conrad Masters," Alex replied.

"Stupid shit," Ferrell muttered to himself.

"So, what's wrong, James?" Alex asked and changed the subject.

"We have a problem. Twenty minutes ago, we had a slave barge crash in the southern hemisphere," the Slave Lord replied and turned back to the terminal.

Concern filled Alex's face as he moved past Ferrell and looked over the sensor readings.

"Any idea why?" the Energy-Caster questioned.

Ferrell merely shook his head.

"Cargo-manifest?" he requested.

Ferrell pulled out a small data-pad and handed it to Alex.

"Gods… Three rogue Tuskerons, five Humans, and a half dozen Accarens," Alex muttered to himself as he looked over the list.

"I have a dropship prepped and waiting for you on landing pad eight. Get out there and clean this up," Ferrell stated firmly.

"Why do I have a feeling your about to tell me the bad news?" Alex questioned.

A smirk swept over Ferrell's face at his friend's pessimistic nature.

"You'll have a slave transport in thirty minutes, but we won't have a barge for a few hours," the Slave Lord replied.

"Oh fantastic," Alex blurted out.

"Load up the Humans and Accarens. As for the Tuskerons, secure them until the barge gets there."

Alex nodded in agreement and turned to leave the tactical center.

"Come on, Cammy. No rest for the wicked," Alex said and tried a new nickname.

Cameron turned and followed Alex down the stairs and out to the powerlift. The door slid shut, and the elevator started a rapid ascent to landing pad eight.

"Pop quiz, what are the differences between the Tuskeron breeds?" Alex said and broke the uncomfortable silence.

Cameron looked down at the floor and tried to recall what she remembered from school.

"Rhinos are the most common and generally work as mercenaries. Lion hybrids are leaders," she paused as she tried to remember the third.

"Buffalo!" Cameron exclaimed.

"And what is unique about them?" he pressed.

Cameron thought about the question but was unsure.

"Don't they also work as mercenaries?" she tentatively asked.

"They can, but buffalo are unpredictable and very dangerous," he clarified.

The door opened, and they walked with haste to the awaiting dropship. The vessel was rectangular, with a dorsal fin arch from front to back. There were four massive engines. Two on the front with the others on the back. Alex and Cameron walked up the metal ramp and into the ship. There was a single Tuskeron pilot in the cockpit with six other guards sitting back to back in the center of the dropship. They each wore a thick leather harness with a thick cable that extended to a pully above them. This allowed the pilot to drop troops without having to risk landing the ship.

Cameron looked down and saw her cloak neatly folded on her chair.

"I had it brought for you," Alex stated and took his seat.

Cameron nodded in reply. She put on the shroud and took a seat next to Alex in a Human sized chair. Their backs were facing the pilot, giving them a perfect view of the six Tuskerons in front of them.

Cameron watched her mentor secure his harness and copied the same process. The hatch sealed, and the dropship lifted off the pad with a lurch. The engines boomed as the vessel rapidly sped toward the crash site. The ship was void of windows, with red lights dimly shining overhead.

"What's your strategy?" one of the Tuskerons asked.

"Secure the crash site and create a perimeter. I want the slaves rounded up and held in a staging area away from the barge," Alex commanded.

"Thirty seconds," the pilot interjected and informed them the drop zone was coming up.

The ship came to a halt and the overhead lights turned green. A split second later, the guards' chairs dropped out from underneath them and the metal cables snapped tight. The pullies squealed as they lowered the thousand-pound hybrids to the sand below.

"Deep breath," Alex said.

Before Cameron could respond, her seat dropped and allowed the cable to take over. It steadily lowered her and after a few seconds Cameron's boots touched down against the sand. She disconnected her harness and observed her surroundings.

Cameron immediately turned to the barge. There were pieces of debris scattered around the crash site. She gave out a cough upon inhaling the fumes from the burning ship. Cameron looked around and gauged her surroundings. Four of the Tuskerons set up a perimeter around the ship. They rounded up three wounded Humans who had been unable to escape. Alex inspected the vessel with the other two guards directly behind him, weapons raised and aimed at a large breach in the hull.

"Cameron, I need your help," he yelled over.

Cameron ran as fast as she could and was at his side within seconds.

"Follow us in," he said directly, "but I want you in the back."

"Yes, sir," she quietly replied.

Alex smiled and patted her on the shoulder. He lifted his right hand, blue energy swirling around it. He made his way to the door, entered the ship and vanished from sight in the blackness of the barge. The Tuskeron guard followed closely behind Alex and took up a defensive position across the aisle. Once inside, the guard motioned for Cameron to follow. She stepped into the ship and took up position across from the guard.

Cameron peeked around the corner and saw Alex slowly make his way through the cargo bay. The guards moved forward with their weapons fixed on the dark bay ahead. Cameron looked around the corner one final time.

Still clear, she thought to herself.

She raised her hands and walked around the corner. Prepared to defend herself against anything that might be lurking in the shadows. The bay held two different sections. The first compartment had six steel-barred holding cells. She walked down the center of the metal deck plates and saw a lump off to the right in one of the cells. As Cameron walked closer, she realized the lump was the mangled, still burning corpse of a lion-bred Tuskeron.

Cameron put her hand over her face to cover up the smell of the burning fur and flesh. To the left, two of the three cells had broken, allowing whatever was trapped inside to escape. Alex moved to the rear of the first holding bay and inspected the hatch that led into the second section.

Alex attempted to open the solid metal door but was stopped by a fallen beam. He braced his shoulder against the beam and put his weight into it. After a moment, he stopped and shook his head.

"Hey Cameron, do you think you can move this for me?" he asked and was slightly embarrassed he did not think of it sooner.

She smiled and stepped past the Tuskeron. Cameron stretched out her hand and effortlessly lifted the heavy object. She moved it to the side and set it down with a clank against the metal deck plate. Alex inspected the door and motioned for the guard to cover him. He threw the door open, stepped forward and crossed into the second holding bay.

As he did, a figure tackled Alex and both beings fell out of sight off to the right of the door. The guard rushed forward to assist but froze at the sight of five Accarens desperately trying to escape the cargo bay. The rhino roared and stood directly in their path. Two of the slaves stopped in fear of the behemoth. The Tuskeron swept his rifle and threw two of the Accarens into the steel bars of the holding cell.

The Tuskeron reached down and picked up the fifth Accaren with its three-fingered hand. The beast held the Humanoid and slammed it against the deck plate.

Cameron stretched out her hands and took hold of the two remaining slaves. She held them in midair for a split second before she hurled them to the left. They flew into one of the unoccupied cells and rendered them unconscious.

Cameron and the guard turned, ready to face whatever came out next. A blue energy wave rippled past the door as Alex activated his second ascension. Cameron watched his attacker fly past the door and heard the crash on the other side of the second bay. A few seconds of breathless anticipation passed before Alex walked into sight.

"All clear," he said, winded by the experience.

Alex motioned for her to join him. Cameron walked forward and entered the second holding bay. She looked back at the Tuskeron who rounded up the beaten slaves and carried them out of the ship. Cameron walked through the square doorframe and gauged her surroundings. The bay was large and rectangular. The Accaren slave was off to the left, slumped against the wall. In the center of the bay was a pit with two and a half meter high walls.

"During transport, this pit has a shield that expands over the top. Looks like it deactivated during the crash," Alex explained.

Cameron walked up to the edge and peered into the pit. She saw the mangled remains of two Humans who died during the crash. Alex walked over to the downed Accaren. He lifted him off the ground and led the battered slave out of the holding bay. Cameron followed Alex through the forward section and into the blinding afternoon light of Camus's sun. He handed the slave off to an awaiting guard and walked up to the lead Tuskeron.

Cameron stood half a meter behind Alex and strained to look up at the massive alien.

"Head count's done. We're missing two Tuskerons. The second lion, and the buffalo," Alex said in a distraught tone.

"What's the play, boss?" the rhino asked in a deep voice.

"Sargus. You and Cameron hold the slaves until a transport can get here. I'll take Zed and see if we can track down the runaways," Alex replied.

He turned and looked over at Cameron.

"You and Sargus are in charge. Keep your eyes open. Load up the transport and be careful," he said firmly.

"How long will you be gone?" she asked, a bit nervous about being left alone with the massive hybrid.

"I'm not sure. Stay close to Sargus and hitch a ride back to the compound when you're done," he replied honestly.

The Energy-Caster moved with haste and motioned for one of the guards to follow him. They took to a jog and soon left her sight after making their way over a sand dune to the north.

Cameron turned her gaze back to Sargus who looked down at her with his black, stone cold eyes.

"Sit tight girl, the transport should be here in a few minutes," Sargus grunted.

He lumbered over to the Accaren slaves who were rounded up away from the barge.

Cameron walked over to a piece of debris and sat down in the shade. Her mind turned to the events of the day and was still in shock of Alex's actions.

How could he do it? she asked herself.

The memory of the woman's cold dead eyes still haunted her vision. She hated his actions, but the part that truly vexed Cameron was the fact the girl's death was her fault. Although she never touched her, the slave girl's blood was still on her hands. Cameron felt the shame of her cold-blooded murder, as if she had done the deed herself.

A loud hum sounded, and her gaze turned skyward to see a slave transport descend rapidly toward her location. The black armored ship flew down and landed two dozen meters away from the Accaren slaves. Cameron stood up and made her way over to Sargus's location.

With the help of the other guard, Sargus had already rounded up the slaves and moved them in the direction of the dropship. Cameron looked from side to side and saw the three remaining rhinos standing on the perimeter.

Sargus and the second guard marched the Accarens forward and had them stand in a line in front of the hatch. The pilot opened the door and motioned as a sign of readiness.

"One at a time. Move into the transport," Sargus growled.

The first of the slaves entered the ship and was escorted back to one of the holding cells. As the second slave crossed the threshold, her mind felt clouded. She could feel the auras of the Accarens and the Tuskeron guards around her. This aura was new. It felt like a Tuskeron, just… different.

By the time the fourth slave entered the ship, the feeling had grown stronger. It was abundantly clear there were two other Tuskerons nearby. Neither of which felt like the rhino hybrids she had become accustomed to.

"Sargus," she said in a shaky tone and peered up at the behemoth.

His black eyes stared down at her.

"I can feel them," she stammered.

The lead guard did not understand what she was trying to convey and rotated his head in confusion.

"The other Tuskerons, they're close!" Cameron exclaimed.

The beast's eyes opened wide at the news, but before he could warn the others, weapons fire sounded loudly on the north ridge. Her focus instantly shifted and watched one of the guards get shot down by an assault-rifle.

The second guard on the ridge turned to assist but was tackled by a lion-bred Tuskeron. The hybrid had thick fur, razor sharp claws and an orange tinted mane. The massive aliens rolled down the ridge and came to a halt with the cat-hybrid on top. Its jaws clinched tightly around the rhino's throat. The lion shook its head a few times and made sure the guard was dead. The lion lifted his gaze and stared over at Cameron and Sargus, blood still dripping from its jaws. Sargus roared out in anger at the sight of his troops being cut down.

The two remaining Accarens took advantage of the chaos and made a break for it. Sargus threw a right hook and knocked the first Accaren out cold with a single blow. The second slave lunged toward Cameron and landed a heavy hit to her face. Her head whipped to the side and Cameron found herself face down on the sand. Her head was spinning. She felt blood pour out of her mouth and nose. Barely conscious, she looked up at the fleeing slave.

He made it about thirty meters before he was shot in the back. The energy bolt hit the Accaren with such force it nearly blew apart his arm and shoulder on impact. Cameron looked back and saw Sargus. He stood a few meters behind her, weapon aimed at the dead Accaren.

"Stay behind me," he commanded.

Sargus turned his attention back to the attacking rogue Tuskerons. The second guard had moved forward and fired on the lion's position. The lion charged and took a bolt to the shoulder before it reached the second guard's location. They fought over the weapon, each one trying to gain control of the assault-rifle. The lion scratched the rhino's face with his sharpened claws. The guard roared out and released his grip of the assault-rifle. The rhino lurched forward with its head lowered. The beast threw his head up and thrusted his horn into the lion's chest. The cat hybrid roared out in pain before the rhino threw the lion to the ground.

"Go!" Sargus yelled to the pilot.

The transport fired up its engines with a boom. The ship lifted off the ground and sped toward the compound. Weapons fire sounded. Cameron's eyes turned to the ridge where she saw the second rogue Tuskeron. The creature was half man, half buffalo, and held a stolen assault-rifle. The buffalo-hybrid stood around fourteen centimeters taller and appeared to have a bit more bulk then the rhinos. He had large curved horns on either side of his head while snot dripped from his nose.

Caught by surprise, the second guard was overwhelmed by the incoming fire and was thrown to the ground. His blood soaked into the sand. Sargus raised his rifle but was pegged by an energy bolt that impacted his chest.

The ground shook as Sargus hit the sand with a crash. Cameron struggled to her feet, head still spinning. Her nose felt broken. The buffalo noticed Cameron's difficulty and charged forward. Weapon aimed at her. The young Ranger stretched forth her hand and grabbed ahold of the Tuskeron. She lifted the creature off the ground but could barely maintain her telekinetic grip on the alien. She swept her arm to the side and hurled the buffalo into the crashed barge. The Tuskeron rolled to the sand and stood back up hardly fazed.

The Tuskeron charged forward. Her head was pounding, and Cameron felt dizzy. Blood poured out of her broken nose and down her chin. She stood her ground against the sprinting hybrid who stood almost triple her height and ten times her bodyweight.

Cameron focused all her mental energy to contain the hybrid, but he continued and within moments was at her location. The buffalo leapt forward.

In a desperate act to save herself, Cameron stretched out her arms, palms facing outward. In that singular moment, she was able to steer the behemoth to the right, just not far enough. As the buffalo flew past, his closed fist connected with her side.

A sharp crack sounded as Cameron felt at least four ribs break on impact. She was thrown off her feet and landed five meters from her current location. Upon hitting the sand, she screamed out in agony at the top of her lungs and was in so much pain she was unable to move. Still on her back, Cameron looked over at the buffalo who had landed face first in the sand. He stood up, shook his head and lumbered toward her.

"Come," the beast growled with hostile intent.

Cameron tried to back away but could not move. The Tuskeron continued forward and towered over her. From behind, the buffalo took a blow to the head, and collapsed to the sand. Her eyes fell upon Sargus, who stood behind the rogue Tuskeron. The rhino held a large club with blood still dripping from the opened wound in his shoulder. Sargus moved forward, struck the buffalo's head again, which left it unconscious.

Sargus turned back to her and made his way over.

"Are you okay?" he asked in a deep voice.

She tried to answer but could not. She tried keeping her eyes open, but it was no use as she passed out from the pain of her injuries.

* * *

Cameron's brown eyes opened, and she took a pain filled breath. Cameron looked over to the edge of her bed, and saw Alex sitting in a solemn manner. The room was dark with moon light shining in from the balcony.

"Where am I?" she gasped and tried to recall what memories she had.

"You're in your room, Cameron," he replied in a kind tone.

She tried to sit up but fell back on to the bed.

"Easy, little one, you took quite the beating. Four broken ribs, a broken nose, and a concussion," he explained.

"How long was I out?" she asked and rubbed her face.

"About four hours. Once we got you back here, the medical staff applied Advanced Healing Compound," he continued referring to the healing gel, "you should be good as new in a week."

His kind words did not change her mood.

"I'm so sorry I failed. I should have been able to stop them," she blurted out.

Alex just shook his head.

"No, Cammy, the faults on me. I should have known they would double back. The good news is you're alright," he replied and looked at the ground.

Silence followed his statement. She turned her gaze and stared at the adjacent wall. Noticing something was wrong, Alex rested his hands in his lap and leaned forward.

"What's on your mind, Cameron?" he asked.

Cameron did not answer and looked at the bed.

"I promise this is a safe place. What's bothering you?"

Cameron was not sure how to phrase the question, and stuttered a few times before getting it out.

"Why did you kill that poor woman in the bazaar?" Cameron spat out with less eloquence then she would have preferred.

Alex put his hands over his face, took a deep breath to focus his thoughts.

"You didn't even ask her any questions or get a confirmed answer on what she really saw," she said in a frustrated tone.

"Cameron, I've already explained her side of this, but think about it this way," Alex replied in a methodical manner, "in that moment I felt I had to make a choice. It was between you and her. Well, to be honest, I'm going to pick you every time. It doesn't matter if there were a dozen Humans, I'd still make the same choice."

His tone was firm and unyielding.

Cameron sat, silenced by his blunt answer.

"What makes me so different from her?" she questioned.

"She was only Human," he answered and hinted toward a dislike of their less evolved cousins.

"What if she had been a Ranger?" she retorted.

"Then we would most likely be having a different conversation," Alex replied honestly.

"Why do you not like them?" Cameron pressed and tried her best to understand his prejudice.

Alex paused and carefully considered his response.

"As an Infiltrator, I worked closely with the Human Republic. My time on New Earth taught me a very valuable lesson," he said referring to his rank in the Ranger military,

"And what was that?" she questioned.

"I learned Humans are just as corrupt, if not more so than our own people."

"But you work for James Ferrell, a Slave Lord," Cameron retorted sharply and pointed out the hypocrisy of his statement.

"You're right, Cameron. I buy and sell slaves. I protect a man like Ferrell, but the work I do is honest," Alex said to her surprise.

"Honest?" Cameron questioned, almost at the point of disbelief.

Alex sat calmly. He leaned forward and kept eye contact.

"In the time you have known me. Have I ever lied, been dishonest about my role here or the work I do?"

Cameron thought about the question long and hard. He was right, as much as she hated to admit it. Alex had been completely transparent.

"No," she finally said.

Alex smiled, and took to his feet.

"Get some sleep, Cammy," he said walking to the door.

He exited the room and left her alone with her thoughts, and the mystery of who Alex Sheridan truly was.

AMBIGUITY OF SHERIDAN

During the two months after the incident at the barge, Cameron began a daily training regimen. Every morning, before the sun peeked over the horizon the young Ranger was already on her way to her first class. Ferrell had personal tutors for a variety of subjects. Her first class was general education. History, math, culture of different races and other subjects. This was the same style of education she would have received on Zail or Agron and gave her a deeper understanding of the aliens who inhabited Known-Space.

For example, Turkcanon anatomy, a sharp blow to their second heart would kill the reptile instantly. Another example, Accarens could handle three times the amount of pain compared to a Human or a Ranger. After she finished her lessons, Cameron entered combat training with Alex. She was instructed in a multiplicity of martial-arts and different forms of fighting styles. Cameron learned the Art of Tirek, and Aries. Both were ancient forms used by the Accarens. Cameron also learned the Style of Shee'ta - Turkcanon swordplay. She was trained in Human kick boxing and Human jujitsu.

From her own people, the combat was split up into two different categories. All Rangers were trained in the form of Shindie. Once they passed the first stages Rangers were split up into two different categories. The first was Agro-Form, this was meant for Shield-Techs, Tanks, and

Ranger-Teleporters. It was an aggressive style of fighting. The second was Caster-Form and was a defensive style of combat. Alex compared it to Human Aikido. Unlike others her age, Cameron was trained in both forms.

After that she had a short break and was off to Ranger training. This was her favorite class. She had one on one time with Alex and had an opportunity to practice her abilities.

This routine was her life and everyday was the same grueling cycle.

One day, she stood in the main sparring room. There was a blue pad on the floor that covered two thirds of the room. Cameron was barefoot with a short pair of gym shorts and a white t-shirt. Her black and silver shroud fit tightly and concealed her face from view.

A female Accaren stood across from her and was close to Cameron's age. The Accaren had thick, black cornrows which were pulled back. She had dark toned skin and had two green rectangles tattooed under each eye. The girl's fists were raised with her gaze fixed on Cameron. The young Ranger turned and looked over at her mentor. He stood at the edge of the mat with his arms crossed.

For the past few days Alex had changed up her training routine. He had instructed Cameron to wear her shroud during combat. Cameron found the practice difficult and overall frustrating. The cloak was lightweight but the hood impaired and narrowed her vision. Inside the lining of the hood were a half dozen holo-emitters which darkened the upper half of her face. From the inside, the emitters gave the wearer clarity and lightened the surrounding area.

Alex stood in silence with an emotionless gaze upon his brow.

"Begin," he commanded.

Cameron's eyes darted back to the Accaren, who had started moving toward her. She matched the girl's pace, fists raised ready to strike. The Accaren threw a jab, but Cameron blocked the incoming attack and weaved to the side. She immediately countered with a left cross and hit the Accaren in the nose.

The girl stumbled back. She quickly recovered and landed a heavy hit to Cameron's chest. The Ranger let out a sharp pain filled gasp and stumbled back. Before she could recover the female slave lunged forward and landed a heavy hit to Cameron's cheek. She lost her balance and fell back on to the blue pad.

"Keep your guard up, Cammy," Alex instructed.

She stood back up, wiped the blood from her lips and retook her stance.

"Begin," Alex said and started the second round.

Cameron bit her lip and glared over at the female slave who had returned to her original location. There was a brief pause before her opponent boldly charged forward. Cameron met her halfway and opened with a jab. The Accaren blocked the hit and weaved to the left outside her visual range. Cameron turned to face her, but the slave moved again and used the blind spots on Cameron's hood against her.

The Ranger became more and more frustrated. She turned again, but this time the dark haired Accaren was waiting for the reaction. The Accaren swung with a right hook and leveled Cameron. The Ranger spun around and slammed into the mat. Blood poured out of her mouth and nose, forming small pools on the pad.

"Did I hurt you, Ranger bitch?" the Accaren sneered.

In her mind something snapped. Cameron stood up in anger, picked up the Accaren with her telekinesis and threw her across the sparring room. The girl flew forward into the far wall and crashed down onto the floor.

"Cameron!" Alex's voice boomed.

The Accaren stood up enraged by the Ranger's act of cheating.

"Parafek! Give me a set of armor and we'll see who wins next," the Accaren threatened.

"Enough. We're done for today," Alex commanded and stood between them.

The Accaren stepped forward, her scornful eyes still locked on Cameron.

"I said we're done! The guards will take you back to your cell," the Energy-Caster's voice thundered at her challenging actions.

The girl spit in Cameron's direction and made her way to the door.

"I hate Rangers," the Accaren muttered to herself.

After the door shut, Cameron walked away from Alex, and sat down on the edge of the mat. Soon after, he sat down next to her. She took off the hood and looked up at him. Her face was badly bruised with dried blood along the edge of her mouth. The left side of her face swelled and clouded her vision.

Alex noticed her pain. He stood up and made his way to the first-aid station on the other side of the room. He picked up a small container of Advanced Healing Compound and retook his seat next to her.

"What's bothering you?" he asked.

Alex opened the container and lightly rubbed a small amount of the AHC on her face.

"It's frustrating, the hood limits my vision," Cameron ranted.

Alex spread more gel over her face and split knuckles.

"So, let me ask you this, why do you need to wear the cloak?" he questioned in a methodical tone.

"It hides my identity," she quickly replied.

It reminded her of the poor girl killed two months before, after seeing her abilities.

"Correct," he replied.

"If I'm wearing this," she started and pointed down at the shroud, "why can't I use my ascension?"

Alex smiled at the question. He put the container of AHC down and rested his hands in his lap.

"You bring up an interesting question, Cammy. Our people over the years have become dependent on their abilities. This is a weakness and overall, I feel this is one of the main reasons why the Ranger Empire will lose the Draith war," he explained, "I promise you Cammy, there will be times where you can't use your abilities. This is something you HAVE to learn."

Cameron gazed down at the ground and nodded in compliance.

"Don't worry, you're getting there," he stated and patted her on the back.

Alex stood up and returned the container to the first-aid station.

"I know," she finally replied, still a bit angry at the situation.

"Come on Cammy, let's go get some lunch. How does Manny's sound?" he asked.

Alex referred to the Human run establishment on the far side of the slave bazaar.

"That sounds amazing!" she exclaimed with a cheerful smile.

Cameron pulled the hood back up and shrouded her face from sight. She took to her feet and followed Alex. They left the sparring room, made their way out of the compound and into the slave bazaar. From there they walked down the promenade and a few minutes later stood at the entrance to Manny's. The restaurant was small and next to the large wall of the fortress.

They walked into the building. It was run-down with tables equally spaced around the front room. The owner of the restaurant stood behind a counter, which was near the kitchen.

"What can I get you both," the man asked.

"Just our usual Joe," Alex replied.

"I'll have it right out, Sheridan," the owner stated and made his way into the kitchen.

They walked over and took a seat next to the wall. Although the place looked old, it had some of the best food on Camus. The Humans referred to it as Mexican cuisine.

"It's quiet in here today," Cameron commented at the lack of customers.

"Yeah, except for that Turkcanon over there, we're all by ourselves," he replied.

Alex nodded to a cloaked figure in the corner. Cameron followed his gaze and looked over at the alien who was back was toward them. He was wearing an authentic Turkcanon Consortium shroud, with orange tribal markings on it. As she looked closer Cameron realized the aura was not Turkcanon. Cameron turned back to Alex with confusion.

"But he's Human," she whispered.

Alex's eyes darted back to the figure and worry filled his expressions.

"Something's wrong. How many Humans are nearby?" he replied with concern.

Cameron closed her eyes and focused on her second Ranger ascension.

"Four other Humans," she replied after a moment.

"We need to leave. Just like we practiced, Cammy. Defensive posture Sigma-Two," Alex replied and reminded Cameron of her Ranger training.

They stood up cautiously and proceeded to the door. Cameron noticed the cloaked figure take to his feet and heard a grenade roll across the floor.

"Wave-nade!" Alex yelled.

The Human Republic manufactured wave technology. It originally came from Old Earth. It was a circular energy-wave with a preset range. It could cut through stone, flesh or any other material. Alex grabbed a hold of Cameron's arm and pulled her to the ground. A split second later, Alex activated his fourth ascension and created an energy bubble around them. The grenade went off with a slash and a deep blue energy-wave erupted from the weapon. It spread and cut through the wall, door and a table.

Alex clenched his jaw as the cutting energy impacted against the shield. Once the blast had subsided, Alex stood up and with one fluid motion fired an energy punch. It hit the cloaked figure directly in the chest, knocked him down and threw him back to the counter.

Cameron made it back to her feet, hands raised palms outward. Her mentor lifted his arm and erupted an energy shield across the center of the restaurant and separated them from the figure. The Human stood up and removed the Turkcanon shroud revealing DX-29 Human Commando armor.

It was black with silver stripes running down the sides. The advanced suit was equipped with Kinetic Energy Stabilizers that created a barrier between the suit and the user. It was air-tight with a built-in oxygen filtration system, anti-gravity harness and was almost the same density as Accaren Infiltrator armor. This gave the Humans an equal chance against the stronger aliens in a one on one fight.

The commando reached back and pulled an HT-62 scatter gun forward, which was on a sling around his shoulder. Cameron's gaze turned to the kitchen where she watched three additional commandos walk forward into the light with their weapons raised. The lead Human, who stood in the center of the group and signaled for his men to stop and hold their position. He stepped forward and carried an enforcer-class battle-rifle. As Cameron looked closer, she could see Captain's bars on the right side of his armor.

"Captain Alex Sheridan," the lead commando said as the microphone in his helmet masked his voice, "fifth ascension Energy-Caster and former Infiltrator for the Ranger Empire."

"Who are you?" Alex asked, but the commando shook his head, disappointed by the Rangers answer.

"Thought you would recognize me, Sheridan. Considering how much time you spent with my wife."

Cameron looked up at her mentor with surprise, but Alex continued his emotionless stare.

"Captain Logan Masters. Last I heard you had a dishonorable discharge and were wanted by the Human Republic. Vigilante was the exact term used," Alex replied after a moment.

"They asked me to return to help with a bigger issue – you," Logan replied and pointed at the Energy-Caster, "did you know your number two on Known-Space's most wanted list, and number one for the Ranger Empire? They hate you almost as much as I do."

"Are you here to arrest me?" Alex questioned.

"No. I'm here to kill you," Logan replied with what sounded like a smile under his helmet.

"We'll see how that play's out for you, Masters," Alex scoffed.

The commando shook his head and an eerie silence followed.

All at once, the commandos opened fire on Alex's shield. Dozens of energy bolts pounded against the barrier and rippled on impact. Cameron could see the strain in Alex's eyes as he supported the field. She turned her focus back to their attackers and lifted both commandos on either side of the Human Captain off the ground. They hung in midair for a moment before she slammed them into the floor. Cameron lifted the Human's again, but this time she threw them into the kitchen, beyond her vision.

Captain Masters and the fourth commando gazed at one another obviously surprised by the past event. Alex used the confusion to his advantage. He lowered the shield and launched an energy punch that hit Captain Masters in the chest. The energy attack leveled the Human officer and threw him back against the wall.

"Captain!" the fourth commando yelled with concern. He turned his attention back to Alex and raised his tactical scatter-gun. Cameron stretched forth her hand once again. She lifted the Human off the ground and threw him in to the kitchen via the back wall.

"Fall back!" Captain Masters yelled to the rest of his team.

Logan made it back to his feet and pulled out an HT-16 energy-pistol strapped to his leg. He pressed a button on the side of the weapon and changed the mode. He fired two stun-bolts into Cameron's chest. She yelped out in pain and dropped to her knees. Her body tensed, and her arms went numb. Alex stepped in front of her and raised a defensive shield.

The Human Captain switched the mode and fired at the energy barrier. He put both hands on the weapon and started moving forward continually firing. After a few steps, Captain Masters was within two meters of their location. Alex lowered the shield and gave the commando the opening he was looking for.

The Human officer pulled the trigger and fired an energy bolt which hit Alex in the shoulder. Alex yelled out in pain and activated his second ascension. A shockwave erupted from his body which threw Masters, Cameron and the surrounding furniture to the outskirts of the medium sized room. She slid across the cold floor and ended up next to the front door. Her eyes darted back to the Human Captain who was still recovering on the opposite side of the restaurant. Alex braced himself and powered up a massive energy burst.

"Hammer!" Alex yelled and activated his fifth ascension.

The blue energy flew forward and hit Captain Masters directly in the chest. The breaking of bones sounded. The Human officer was hit with such force he flew through the sandstone wall and rolled across the dirt filled street.

"You okay, kid?" Alex asked, and helped Cameron to her feet.

The front door flew open. Four rhino-bred Tuskerons rushed in with their weapons raised and secured the main room.

"They went that way," Alex said and pointed toward the kitchen.

Alex turned his attention back to the wounded Captain and walked through the gaping hole in the building. Cameron followed and squinted as she adjusted her eyes to the bright light. Cameron looked down at the commando who crawled across the earth. He moved forward slowly and tried to reach his energy-pistol. Alex stepped in front of the Human and kicked the weapon away. Hearing footsteps, she turned back to the street and saw two Tuskerons approach.

"Put him in a holding cell on the main level," Alex commanded, "and make sure he is under heavy guard."

The guards walked forward, picked up the broken man and carried him back in the direction of the compound. Alex and Cameron turned and made their way back into the restaurant. They walked up to the lead guard and waited for a report.

"The Humans escaped through a hidden passage in the back. It leads to a tunnel that goes under the wall," the rhino said in a gruff voice.

"Damn. Any sign of where they went?" he asked. The Tuskeron shook his head.

"Keep searching, I'll be in the fortress if you need me," the Energy-Caster continued.

Alex and Cameron left the restaurant, made their way back through the bazaar and into the safety of the fortress. Alex walked briskly with Cameron on his heels.

"Sheridan!" a voice thundered behind them.

Cameron turned back and saw Ferrell with two guards rapidly approach. Alex turned back and made his way over to the Slave Lord.

"James," he replied in an emotionless tone.

"I heard what happened. What's your next move?" Ferrell asked.

"I'm going to have a talk with Logan Masters," Alex replied in a blunt tone.

"Good. Get the answers we need," the Slave Lord said.

Alex crossed his arms, surprised by Ferrell's answer.

"You're not joining the interrogation?" he asked.

"No. I've been summoned by the Ninth Faction Council, should only be gone for a few days. Hold down the fort until I get back," Ferrell replied and continued toward the landing pad.

"Oh, and I want Cameron with you when you interrogate Masters," he started and turned back to face them.

"James—"

"Not an option," Ferrell retorted.

He continued his journey and soon left their sight.

Alex put his hands over his face and took a deep breath.

"Are you okay?" Cameron asked and saw the distress in his expressions.

She looked over and saw his shoulder injury. Burned and untreated.

"You should have someone look at that," the female Ranger continued and pointed at the wound.

"I'll be fine. Right now, we have work to do," Alex said bluntly after a few seconds.

He turned and took off in the direction of where the Human Captain was being held. She quickly followed and soon stopped at a solid metal door. There were two Tuskerons outside and held their weapons tightly. Alex looked down and brought himself to Cameron's level. He knelt in silence for a moment. She looked into his light blue eyes and saw an intensity she had never seen before. Cameron readjusted her hood nervously and waited for him to speak.

"Understand, Cameron…I don't want you to see what's about to happen, but clearly I have little choice in the matter. Here are the rules: Stay in the back, keep your cloak on, and stay quiet," he said in a stern tone.

Cameron lowered her head and nodded slightly. Alex saw her distress and put his hand under her chin. Cameron's mind froze as she looked into his kind eyes. He then took off her hood.

"No matter what happens, no matter what he says, I will always be here for you," Alex said in a calmer tone.

"Yes, sir," she replied, not sure of what to think of his honest statement.

Cameron pulled up her hood and made sure it fully covered her face. Alex took to his feet and typed in the security code into the control panel. The lock clicked. The door swung inward and opened into a medium sized room. Logan was in the center. He sat in a chair with his hands bound tightly behind his back. His armor and shirt had been removed. As Cameron looked closer, she saw massive bruising around the Human's chest where Alex's energy-hammer had impacted him.

They walked into the interrogation room and Cameron stood in the back next to the door. To her left was a first aid station and a small table with two metal chairs around it. To the right was a large table that had Logan's armor and weapons spread out over it.

Captain Masters was well built and had multiple scars over his chest and arms. He had light brown hair with deep brown eyes. There were two Tuskerons standing behind him. Alex motioned for the guards to leave. They left the interrogation room, shut the door and locked them inside.

"Hello Logan," Alex said calmly.

He walked over to the first aid station and pulled out a jar of AHC. As he made his way back, Alex opened the small container and started applying it to his wounded shoulder.

"You must be terrified of me to bring a child into an interrogation. Do you want her to stand and watch as you torture me?" Logan taunted.

Alex did not respond to his question. He picked up one of the metal chairs and set it down with the back facing the commando. The Energy-Caster took a seat and rested his arms against the back of the chair.

"So, Captain, who sent you and your team here?" Alex asked.

Logan stayed silent.

"Was it the Human Republic? Or did the Rangers send you?" he asked again.

The Human Captain remained silent. Alex stood up and moved the chair to the side. He turned back to his prisoner and fired a small energy burst into Logan's broken ribs. Cameron jumped, and her stomach turned as Logan yelled out in pain.

"Who sent you?" Alex yelled with more intensity.

Logan grit his teeth and refused to answer. Alex fired a stronger burst and put the Human in even more pain.

"Screw off, Sheridan," Logan screamed.

"Give me what I want!" Alex yelled and fired another burst.

Logan slumped his head and was at the point of hyperventilating. Alex walked forward and stood in front of the brutalized Human.

"I remember the first time you came over for dinner. I never liked Rangers, but my wife thought the world of you," Logan recalled, "she loved you like a brother and you slaughtered her like an animal."

"Would you like to know why Michelle died? Do you want to know what happened to your wife?" Alex questioned.

"You murdered her in cold blood, you son of a bitch! What else do I need to know?" Logan yelled back.

"Yes, yes I did. Do you want to know why?" he pressed.

"And what if I did?" Logan growled.

"Then all you have to do is tell me who sent you," Alex replied.

The Energy-Caster stood, paced back and forth and kept eye contact with Logan.

"It's not like I asked you for fleet positions or access codes. All I want to know is who sent you. And let's say it is the Ranger Empire, why do you care? You hate Rangers in general," he continued and tried to invoke the Human's prejudice.

"Oh, but they hate you almost as much as I do," Logan admitted.

Alex stopped dead in his tracks and turned back to the commando.

"It was the Empire? But why would they send you and not one of their own teams?" Alex replied, consumed with his own thoughts.

Logan did not respond. The Energy-Caster started pacing again as he tried to work through the puzzle that had been presented. After a moment, his facial expressions changed as if a light-bulb had gone off in his mind.

"Because the Rangers can't openly engage the Ninth Faction. It would be an act of war. The Ranger Empire can't afford to fight a war on two fronts, not while they're engaged with the Draith," he thought out loud and put the puzzle together.

"Did Arland assign you, or was it Lancaster?" Alex asked.

Logan did not respond.

"Doesn't matter, you've told me what I needed to know for now. So, here's my end of the bargain," Alex said.

He retrieved the chair and placed it once again in front of Logan. The Energy-Caster took a seat and rested his arms on the back of the chair.

"After I stole the fleet locations and code names for the Human infiltrator teams. The Human Republic dropped Michelle and I off on Oc'tal'ia. I was on my way to meet the buyer when your wife confronted me. She had figured it out. As we argued, Ninth Faction forces surrounded us," Alex explained.

He paused and took a deep breath. Cameron could hear the pain and sorrow in his voice as he recalled the memories.

"I had a choice to make, Logan. Either let the slavers have her. Which I knew they would torture her for information and then kill her. Or option two, give her a quick death. I chose the latter," he confessed.

"She trusted you! And you murdered her!" Logan screamed, outraged by the explanation and spit at Alex.

The Energy-Caster stood up and wiped his face. He turned and walked back toward the door. He reached for the control, then paused.

"I loved your wife. She was my partner, and my friend. Nothing pains me more."

"I hate you!" Logan screamed in response and nearly foamed at the mouth.

Alex opened the door and Cameron followed him out.

"I will kill you, Sheridan! I don't care how long it takes me. I'll find you!" the Human Captain screamed as Alex shut and sealed the door.

He walked over to the Tuskeron guard who stood off to the side.

"I want him placed under heavy guard. Four outside and two inside the holding room," Alex commanded.

"Understood," the behemoth replied.

Cameron followed Alex down the hallway and stopped once they were out of earshot of the guards. She took off her hood. He knelt in front of her and studied her young face.

"Are you okay?" he asked.

"Is it true?" she questioned, still a bit nauseous from the past events.

"Every word," he replied honestly.

"Could you ever...do that to me?" Cameron stuttered almost at the point of tears.

A look of sorrow filled her mentor's expressions as the words left her lips.

"Oh, Cammy, I'd fight to my last breath before I would let anything happen to you," he replied. Alex stood back up and put his hand on his wounded shoulder.

"Go get some rest, little one. Good job today."

"Thank you," she responded with a half-smile.

Cameron made her way back to her room, cleaned up, and rested her head on the soft pillow. Her thoughts were filled with the day's events. She now knew the secrets behind Alex's actions in joining Ferrell, or at least some of them. It explained why Captain Masters hated him, but not why he left or betrayed his oath to the Ranger Empire. Exhausted, she closed her eyes and fell into a deep sleep.

* * *

Cameron's eyes flashed open and sat straight up in bed. The young Ranger was out of breath and sweat rolled down her forehead.

"Ranger," Cameron gasped, overcome by the aura she felt, "there's another Ranger in the fortress!"

Cameron jumped out of bed. She put on her shroud and covered her shorts and tank top. She laced up her boots faster than she had ever done in the past and rushed out the door at top speed. A minute later, she skidded to a stop and pounded on Alex's door.

Alex answered after a moment and appeared to be half asleep. His gaze shifted down to Cameron and surprise filled his face.

"What's wrong, Cammy?" he asked instantly seeing something was amiss.

"There's another Ranger in the compound! I can sense him," she exclaimed and created panic in her mentor's expressions.

"We need to go," Alex replied.

He reached back into the roof and pulled his leather jacket off its hook. he forcefully shut the door and put his coat on mid stride. The pair took off in a dead sprint for the interrogation room. They rounded the final corner and stopped dead in their tracks.

All four Tuskeron guards were on the ground, each killed by close range weapons fire. Cameron followed Alex to the door as he opened it. Inside the room, both guards Alex had assigned were also dead.

"Damn it," Alex cursed, upon seeing Captain Masters had escaped.

"Sheridan," the gruff voice of a Tuskeron sounded over the comm.

Alex pulled the device from his belt and lifted it to his mouth.

"Yes?" he replied

"We have intruders on landing pad six. They've landed a ship and have engaged our forces," the guard explained.

"On our way," Alex replied.

He hooked the comm back to his belt and took off at top speed for the landing pad. They ran down the hallway, up two sets of stairs and stopped outside the entrance to the platform. There were guards on either side of the door frame. Their assault-rifles raised and firing out toward the landing pad. Alex fearlessly stepped around the corner and raised a blue energy barrier. The guards stopped their fire and held their position. Cameron followed her mentor and gazed out onto the circular landing pad.

There was a small, jet black transport with three Human commandos taking cover around it. Her eyes fell on Captain Masters who was being helped toward the ship. The female Ranger helping him had a thin petite build with short blond hair.

"Stop!" Alex commanded.

Logan and the mysterious woman turned at the sound of his voice.

"Hello, Sheridan," she said in an emotionless tone.

"Captain Amber Young. I was wondering if the Empire had the balls to send an Infiltrator," Alex replied.

"Let us go, Alex. Or you'll have to deal with me," she threatened in a firm tone.

"I'll take that bet!" Alex yelled back.

He dropped the shield and threw an energy burst at the pair. Amber disappeared and allowed the energy punch to hit Logan. It slammed into his shoulder and threw him to the ground. A second later, Amber teleported directly in front of Alex. She landed a three-punch combo and threw the Energy-Caster off balance. Alex fought, but the Ranger woman continued to teleport around him, landing punch after punch. She appeared behind Alex, grabbed ahold of him and vanished from sight.

"Alex!" Cameron screamed but he was nowhere to be seen.

She turned her attention back to Logan who crawled across the pad.

"Open fire," she commanded.

The Tuskerons followed Cameron's orders and dozens of energy bolts flew over the platform.

"Get the Captain," one of the Humans yelled.

A female commando stepped out from behind the ship. She made it to Logan and helped him to his feet. Two energy bolts impacted the wall next to Cameron. Her head whipped in the direction of the incoming fire and saw the other two commandos target her location. Cameron stretched out her hands and lifted them off the ground. She suspended both men in mid-air as she walked out onto the platform.

She threw her hand to the side, hurling one of the commandos off the landing pad. The Human slammed into the outer wall and plummeted over a hundred meters to the sands below. Still holding the second Human, Cameron raised him higher. She used all her strength and crashed him against the landing pad.

"Go!" the commando yelled back to his comrades.

He stood up and drew his energy-pistol. Before he could pull the trigger, Cameron lifted the Human once again and slammed him three separate times into the landing pad. On the third hit a sharp crack sounded as the Human's armor broke. Cameron lifted the lifeless body and tossed him off the pad.

A loud boom sounded as the Human transport's engines fired up. The vessel lifted off the ground and flew away from the compound. The

Tuskerons and the auto-turrets targeted the ship, but the vessel went into stealth and disappeared.

"Shit," Cameron said to herself as she watched Logan escape.

Her attention turned back to her mentor.

"I need a location on Alex," Cameron said to the lead Tuskeron.

The alien pulled out his comm and checked with the tactical center.

"He and the other Ranger are at the base of the wall. Directly below us," he replied after a moment.

Cameron rushed to the edge of the platform and looked over the sands below. Through the darkness she could see flashes of blue from Alex's shield energy.

"We need guards down there ASAP," Cameron ordered, and turned back to the hundred-meter drop off.

You've practiced for this, she thought to herself, *you must help him.*

Without hesitation she fearlessly stepped off the edge and started to freefall to the ground below. The wind whipped through Cameron's hair as she continued her fall. Cameron placed her hands at her sides, palms facing downward. As she approached the ground, Cameron activated her ability and slowed her descent.

She hit the ground with a thud and peered forward. Alex was a few meters away from her. He was on his knees and had been badly beaten by the Ranger-Teleporter. Amber stood directly in front of him, energy weapon aimed at his head. Cameron stood up and took hold of the Ranger with her ascension. She swept her arm to the side and launched Amber into the outer wall of the compound. Cameron rushed over to her mentor and helped him to his feet.

"Are you alright?" she asked, upon seeing his war-torn appearance.

"Been better," he replied honestly.

They turned back to face the teleporter who had just made it back to her feet.

"Well isn't this interesting, how long has Ferrell had a Ranger-Telekinetic?" Amber asked with intrigue.

"That's not your concern, Amber," Alex sharply replied.

"Don't get all protective, Sheridan. You're a damned traitor. You sold out good people and gave away our fleet locations. The Ranger High Council wants you dead and I am more than happy to help with that request," she spouted back rudely, "I will sit at Arland's left hand if I bring back your head. Imagine what they will say when I bring her in."

Amber teleported forward. She clocked Cameron across the jaw and threw the Telekinetic to the ground. Cameron looked up and saw Amber target Alex next. He tried to defend himself with energy blasts but Amber continually dodged and kept teleporting out of the way. She reappeared above him, preparing to issue another heavy blow, but this time Cameron grabbed a hold of her with her telekinetic abilities.

Cameron held her in mid-air and hurled Amber back toward the wall. As Amber flew uncontrollably, she activated her abilities and teleported right in front of Alex. He instinctively raised a blue energy shield between them. Without time to react, Amber slammed into the barrier. The Ranger fell to the ground, stunned by the defensive move. Alex lowered the shield and activated his fifth ascension.

"Hammer!" he shouted and launched a massive burst of energy.

The energy-hammer pounded into Amber's chest and broke most of the bones in her rib cage. She rolled across the sand and stopped ten meters from them.

"Best work, Cammy," Alex said, barely able to stand.

In the distance they could hear gasping. Cameron and Alex made their way to the Ranger-Teleporter. She was lying on her back, blood running down the side of her mouth. She gasped for air. As Cameron looked down at her, she could tell Amber was close to death. Alex bent down and knelt next to his former comrade.

"I'm sorry," he said with a mournful expression.

"Traitor..." she murmured before life left her.

Alex reached forward, shut her eyes and stared at her lifeless body.

"Did you know her?" Cameron asked.

"I did," Alex replied.

He stood up and wiped a single tear from his eye.

"We worked together for a number of years. She was always a good friend," he replied, "what about Logan Masters?"

"He got away," Cameron replied in a frustrated tone.

"It's okay, kid. If it weren't for you and your sense ability, we'd both be dead," he said in a kind tone and patted her on the back.

A hum sounded overhead. Seconds later, a Tuskeron dropship flew down and landed beside them.

"Do you think Captain Masters will come back?" Cameron asked as they walked over to the awaiting ship.

"Not for a while, but if I had to guess. I'd say he'll be showing up at some point in the future," he replied.

They boarded the ship, prepared to face whatever the Rangers, Draith or Humans would send at them next.

ALLIANCE OF THE DAMNED

Alex and Cameron walked through the hallways of the fortress. It had been one year since the Draith had ripped the young Ranger from her home and sold her to the Slave Lord James Ferrell. It was an early morning and the fourteen-year-old felt tired as she made the brisk walk.

They proceeded to the entrance of the throne room and stopped at the closed doors. After a moment, the guards opened the doors and allowed them to enter the beautiful room. They strolled down the stairs and stopped at the base of the hexagon platform. Ferrell sat perched on his wooden throne and seemed excited to see them.

"Good morning," the Slave Lord said in an unusually chipper tone.

"Good morning, James," Alex replied also taken aback by the man's positive behavior.

Ferrell took to his feet and walked down the stairs of the platform.

"Today is a good day," Ferrell stated with a devious smile.

Both Rangers followed him around the platform, down the hallway and into the tactical center.

"So why is today a good day?" Alex questioned.

"Because my friend, today marks the final blow that destroys the all-powerful Ranger Empire," Ferrell proclaimed with pride.

Cameron's gaze turned to Alex who was equally confused by his statement.

"I know the Rangers are losing the war, but for the Draith to conquer Rydon. It would be a blood bath on both sides," Alex replied skeptically.

"True," Ferrell agreed, his arrogant smile remaining.

"What am I missing, James?" Alex pressed in a direct tone.

"As I'm sure you know, the Draith attack fleet has been in a blockade around Auctus. The Rangers greatest military stronghold. Once Auctus falls, the Hunters will have a clear line to strike at Rydon, and they intend to do so. Since the beginning of this war, the Ninth Faction has remained neutral in this conflict. Six months ago, the Draith clans opened negotiations. They want a faster end to the war. I have a shuttle prepped on landing pad three. We'll be going to meet with the Ninth Faction Council and finalize the details of our master plan," Ferrell explained in a sinister tone.

Cameron stood in silence and tried to absorb the information.

In the past year, she had heard more than one reference to the mysterious Ninth Faction Council but had never seen them. Nor visited the hidden council chamber.

"You want Cammy to come too?" Alex asked with surprise as if he were reading her mind.

"Yes, it's time she's introduced to the true power in Known-Space," Ferrell replied.

Ferrell motioned for the Rangers to follow him. They made their way to the powerlift at the rear of the tactical center. The lift doors shut, and the elevator started a rapid ascent to the landing pad above them. The group walked out onto the pad and saw Ferrell's black personal transport. Once they had boarded, the vessel lifted off the ground and set course for the hidden station which housed the council chambers.

Inside the vessel, Cameron took her seat toward the center. She leaned back in the comfortable black leather chair and propped her feet up on the ottoman in front of her. Ferrell sat comfortably at the front of the transport. His thick neck length hair pulled back into a ponytail and had an emotionless look on his face. Her eyes darted back to Alex who stood at a small mini-bar off to her right. He mixed two drinks and made his way back over to Cameron.

"Here you go," he said with a smile and handed her a drink.

It was red and appeared to have a cherry.

"Thank you. What is it?" Cameron asked with a crooked smile.

"The Humans call it a Shirley Temple," Alex replied.

He took a seat next to her and gripped his own glass.

"They were always one of Michelle's favorites," he said and referred to his old partner.

Cameron took a sip of the beverage and gave out a slight cough as the bubbles from the carbonated drink tickled her nose.

"It's really good," she said with a smile and took another sip.

"I'm glad you approve," Alex replied and took a drink of his whisky.

"So, tell me about the Ninth Faction," Cameron inquired and changed the subject.

"Thought you'd never ask," he replied with a smile and took a large sip of his whisky before continuing, "the Ninth Faction started gaining power around twenty years after the end of the Accaren War. The council is made up of the minor powers, can you name them?"

Cameron pondered the question for a moment before she answered.

"Turkcanon Consortium, the Tuskeron Hordes, and the Slave Lords," she replied.

Cameron knew she missed one. She snapped her fingers and desperately tried to remember.

"Narairian Hives!" she exclaimed after a moment.

"Nice work, Cammy. Each race will have one ambassador that will be present at the council meeting," he explained.

"So, does the Ninth Faction have a leader?" she questioned and tried to gain a better understanding.

"They do, and his name is Adrian Quin. He's Human, very old and has abilities," Alex responded.

Cameron gave a crooked glance at the contradictions Alex had brought up.

"He's Human, but he has abilities?" she questioned, almost to the point of disbelief.

"Strange isn't it," Alex replied with a laugh and agreed with her statement.

"So how?" Cameron asked and was drawn into the conversation.

"The rumor is, Adrian's from Old Earth," Alex explained and referred to the Humans lost homeworld deep in the Orion-Cluster.

"Supposedly, a thousand years ago he and a group of friends learned how to control dimensional energy. This gives them abilities, and a very long lifespan," Alex explained.

Cameron took a sip of her drink and tried to imagine the man.

"What is he like?" Cameron asked after a moment.

"He's ruthless and has a short temper. Be careful when you deal with him," Alex warned.

The Energy-Caster's tone put her on edge, but Cameron brushed it off and pressed forward.

"What about the other ambassadors?" Cameron inquired.

"Good question," Alex replied.

He took a sip of his whisky and leaned forward.

"The first is Maglar. Lion-bread Tuskeron and leader of Tawson 4. Second. Yen'Ta representative for the Turkcanon Consortium. The third you already know," he said and nodded over to Ferrell.

"What about the Narairians? What's the name of their ambassador?" Cameron pressed on.

Alex gave out a slight chuckle at the question.

"What's so funny?" she asked with a crooked smile.

"The Narairians are one interesting lot," Alex replied, going deeper into the insectoid race, "they are aggressive and short tempered. In fact, the only reason why they're in the Ninth Faction is because Adrian forced them into it at gun point. I've watched Adrian kill more than one ambassador who was unwilling to follow the instructions of the council," Alex clarified.

This news took the young Ranger by surprise. She leaned forward and played with her drink.

"So, if the Narairians are such an issue, why give them a voice in the council?" Cameron inquired.

"Two reasons. First off there are trillions of the little bastards. The Hives territories starts on the far end of Ninth Faction space and goes deep into Unexplored-Space," Alex explained, "reason number two, although the bugs don't care about the politics or who is in control. They still have one of the largest fleets in all of Known-Space. I've thought about it for a while. The only reason the Ranger Empire has not openly declared war on the Ninth Faction is because they fear retaliation from the Narairians."

"That explains a lot," she replied.

Cameron brought her knees up and turned her gaze to the window. It was a lot for her to take in, but this was the only way to stay alive and find a way to gain her freedom.

* * *

The lights overhead flashed, and the ship shook as it exited subspace. Cameron whipped around and looked out the window.

"Welcome to the Garocus system, Cammy," Alex said and finished off the rest of his drink. Cameron looked out and gazed into the pitch-black system. Ahead she saw an old space station orbiting a dead world. There were four other ships surrounding it. She recognized a Tuskeron warship but had no knowledge of the other three. The shuttle flew forward and docked with the station. Cameron reached down, opened her bag and pulled out her shroud. She put it on and pulled the hood firmly over her head.

The hatch opened, and Ferrell walked out with Alex and Cameron behind him. The station was dark and gloomy. The hallways were large and had water dripping from the ceiling. They made their way through a winding maze and came to a stop at a large circular door.

"Rules," Alex said quietly, "stay quiet unless you are addressed and take up position on Ferrell's left."

Before she could respond Ferrell opened the door and walked into the council chambers. It was a mid-sized room with an oval table in the center. Ferrell walked forward and took his customary seat next to Maglar. On the other side of the table sat the Turkcanon and Narairian ambassadors. Their faces were shrouded by the darkness. A few meters beyond their end of the table hung a spotlight that was pinpointed to a square on the floor. "Welcome Ferrell," a man's voice sounded from the head of the table.

Cameron looked over to where the voice had come from but all she saw was a shadowed figure.

"Thank you, Adrian," the Slave Lord replied.

"So, who's your new bodyguard?" Adrian asked.

Although she could not see his face, Cameron could still feel his piercing eyes on her. Ferrell motioned for her to step forward and answer the question. She moved into the spotlight and took off her hood.

"Well aren't you just a cutie. You're a Ranger if I had to guess?" Adrian commented.

Cameron nodded but was too nervous to speak.

"Show me," Adrian continued with intrigue in his voice.

Cameron glanced over at Ferrell who motioned for her to comply with the order.

She stretched forth her hand and lifted a small glass on the table in front of Adrian. Whispers sounded as she raised the glass to his eye level. Adrian reached forward and took hold of his drink. He took a large chug of the crystalline glass and leaned forward into the dim light over the table.

His appearance caught her by surprise. He was in his late twenties, with a short, thin build. He had sandy blond hair with a small ear-ring in his left ear. He carried himself with pride and had almost a punk style about him. This was opposite to the image Cameron had visualized of the thousand plus year old Human. He had deep brown eyes which stayed locked on her.

"You amaze me, Ferrell," Adrian chuckled to himself.

"I knew you'd approve," Ferrell replied.

"What's your name?" the blond Human inquired.

"Cameron," she answered in a quiet tone.

"Would you like to know a secret, Cameron?" he asked.

"I guess," Cameron replied, unsure of where the conversation was going.

"I knew your predecessor, Simon Cail. He was also known as the last great Telekinetic. I'm sure you've heard of him, right?"

"Yes sir," she replied with a nod of her head.

"And you know his history?" he pressed.

"In the final year of the Accaren War, Simon Cail went insane and slaughtered his entire platoon. He was marked as a traitor by the Ranger High Council and was brought to justice by the Battalion Commander Carson Blake," Cameron replied and quoted Journals of the Accaren War nearly word for word.

"What if I told you all the history books are wrong?" Adrian smirked, "what if I told you that myself and two others were charged with killing the rogue Telekinetic when Carson Blake failed."

Cameron looked back at Alex who shared her confusion toward the statement.

"I don't understand," Cameron admitted.

"The Ranger High Council merely used the Battalion Commander to cover up their gross incompetence. The truth is, the Ranger Empire had no means of stopping Simon Cail and used the power of the Crimson Syndicate to get their way," he explained, "well that was a fun distraction, back to business."

Cameron took a step back into the shadows and put on her hood.

"Where are we at?" Ferrell asked and tried to get caught up.

"Well, we were talking about the risks of our master plan," Adrian replied, "speaking of which, where does the Turkcanon Consortium stand on the subject?"

"The Turkcanon Consortium likes the strategy, but fears retaliation from the Ranger Empire."

"If we succeed there won't be any retaliation," Ferrell retorted.

"I agree with the Slave Lord," Maglar interjected, "once the Humans lose their backing of the Rangers, we'll have the opportunity we've been waiting for. The Tuskeron Hordes vote in favor of selling the hydro-bomb to the Draith."

Cameron's jaw dropped and her eyes opened wide as Maglar spoke. It was a weapon built for one thing, freezing a planet and eradicating all life.

Clicking and popping sounded.

"The Narairians will not work with Draith, hybrid. Nor will they tolerate your arrogance slaver," the alien's translator declared.

"Shut up, Il'ii'ek," Adrian's voice thundered.

Enraged by his quick dismissal, the Narairian leaned forward and slammed his fists against the table. The alien had six legs, green and black armored skin, with a curved sharpened jaw.

"The Hive will not follow this path of destruction, member of the Syndicate," the insect retorted.

Adrian stood up, infuriated by the Narairian's insolence. Red energy swirled and formed around his arm. Adrian threw a right hook and launched a deep red sphere of energy into the insect. The aliens head snapped back and broke the insect's neck with a single blow.

"I despise Narairians," Adrian cursed and sat back down.

"Good work, Adrian. Now you're going to have to send for yet another representative," Ferrell interjected with a chuckle.

"If they weren't so damned aggressive, we wouldn't be having this conversation," Adrian retorted, "now, back to the task at hand. Ferrell, what are your thoughts on the issue?"

"Selling a hydro-bomb to the Draith is going to help us in a variety of ways. The Draith will use this weapon against the Ranger homeworld of Rydon and will bring an immediate end to the war. Second point, the Human Republic will lose the protection of the Rangers, which in turn will give us the push we need to strike and enslave the Human worlds," he said in a well-spoken manner.

The council sat in silence at Ferrell's statement.

"Do you have any other objections, Yen'Ta?" Adrian asked the Turkcanon in a stern voice.

"The Turkcanon Consortium agrees with the plan," the reptile responded and retracted his prior statement.

"Perfect. Ferrell, I'm putting you in charge of negotiations. Head to Peer and pick up the weapon from Castus," Adrian commanded.

"Where are we meeting the Draith?" Ferrell inquired.

"Aathis," the Syndicate member replied, referring to the former Ranger controlled colony located on the border of Ranger and Draith space.

"Maglar, You're in charge of security. Get a fleet of warships and meet Ferrell on Peer," he continued and turned to the Tuskeron.

"Understood," the lion-hybrid replied with a bow of his head.

"We have no room for failure, let's bring an Empire to its knees!" Adrian proclaimed.

With the meeting concluded, Ferrell, Maglar, Cameron and Alex exited the council chamber and made their way back to the transports. Alex walked beside her and had remained silent since the Ninth Faction had revealed their plan. Maglar split off toward his dropship while the other three entered the Human transport. Alex walked over to a chair, took a seat and put his hands over his face. Cameron made her way over to her mentor and sat next to him.

"Are you alright?" Cameron asked with empathy.

"I've been better, Cammy," he replied in a sickened tone.

The ship shook as it undocked from the station. Soon after, the transport set course for Peer and jumped into subspace. Alex stood up, walked over to the mini-bar and poured a straight shot of Human whisky. He downed the drink and immediately made another. Cameron looked over at Ferrell who was also observing Alex's actions.

"Do we need to talk?" Ferrell asked the Energy-Caster.

"The council has reached a decision, what else is there to talk about?" Alex replied and downed the second shot.

"That's not what I asked you, Sheridan," Ferrell retorted.

Alex finished his third drink and turned around to face the Slave Lord.

"Billions of lives, James! Gods, how did we get here?" Alex responded in disbelief.

The Slave Lord walked forward and poured a glass of the same whisky Alex was drinking.

"We've been going down this narrow, God forsaken path for years," Ferrell replied after taking a sip of his beverage.

"We will be branded as the greatest mass murderers of the Draith war—"

"No!" Ferrell yelled back and cut Alex off, "the Draith will take credit for that. History will never hear this conversation or know who gave the Draith the ability to annihilate the Rangers."

"This is an alliance of the damned," Alex replied and lowered his head.

"Considering the Rangers used this same military strategy to end the Accaren war, I find the irony fitting," the Slave Lord argued.

"Billions of lives, James," Alex retorted and repeated his prior statement.

"The Ninth Faction needs the Ranger Empire out of the way. A hydro-bomb in Draith hands is the fastest way to reach that goal," Ferrell protested.

Alex poured another drink and made his way back to his seat.

"I know, James. It's just messed up," he finally replied in a sickened tone.

Ferrell walked past them and made his way to his office which was located at the rear of the ship. After the Slave Lord was out of earshot, Alex let out a deep sigh.

"You've been quiet. What do you have to add?" he said and turned his attention to Cameron.

Cameron thought about the question for a moment before she answered.

"Are we really going to do this?" she quietly asked, "are we really going to destroy our people's homeworld?"

Alex chuckled and downed another drink.

"For the first time, kid, you and I stand on the same ground. Neither one of us has a choice in the matter," Alex replied.

Cameron could hear the frustration in his voice. She decided to drop the subject and turned her gaze back to the mesmerizing blue rings of subspace.

* * *

It did not take them long to reach their destination. Soon after exiting subspace, Cameron moved to the window and looked out at Peer. There were a dozen Tuskeron warships patrolling the space around the brownish tinted world.

Years ago, Peer was part of the Human Republic, but after the Ninth Faction started their campaign and the Slave Lords took power. Peer became part of the Ninth Faction. Soon after, they enslaved the population and turned it into the largest weapons dump in all of Known-Space.

The transport flew past the armada and down to Castus's compound. Castus was Human. He had been appointed by the Ninth Faction many years before to support and maintain the planet. The transport touched down on the landing pad with a jolt. Ferrell made his way back into the main section of the ship and walked to the hatch. Alex and Cameron joined him and a second later the door opened. Cameron followed both down the ramp and observed her surroundings.

There were crates and boxes as far as the eye could see, with a twisted walkway that spread through the stockpile of weapons. Her eyes turned back to Ferrell who stood in front of a ten-story building. As they waited, a heavy-set man walked out the front door, with two Turkcanon guards behind him.

"Is that Castus, or the man who ate him?" Cameron heard Alex whisper to Ferrell.

"He's got to be over three hundred pounds," Ferrell replied under his breath.

"He's half the size of a full grown Tuskeron," Alex countered.

The Slave Lord chuckled at the comment and simply shrugged.

"Ferrell, welcome to Peer," Castus said with a cough.

The Slave Lord walked forward and shook his hand.

"Castus, I see life is treating you well," Ferrell said and pointed at the man's gut.

Castus gave out a hardy laugh at Ferrell's jest.

"I have all the food, wine, and parafeks a man could hope for," Castus boasted and continued to laugh.

Cameron could not help but roll her eyes at the man's filth and gluttony. She had heard stories about his lust and greed, but his depraved nature had already passed her expectations.

"Come my old friend, let us head back to my office while your people load up the weapon. I have some A'Zealion wine I want you to try," he proclaimed.

Castus clapped his hands together and one of the Turkcanons stepped closer to Alex and Cameron.

"En'Te will show you to the weapon," the obese man decreed.

Castus immediately turned his attention back to Ferrell and both men walked into the building.

"Lead the way," Alex said to the guard.

"Follow me," the reptile replied in a deep voice.

They turned and made their way through the maze of crates. Along the way Cameron saw a variety of weapons and equipment. There were stacks of Tuskeron assault-rifles, energy-pistols, Human attack craft and artillery platforms. They traveled by hundreds if not thousands of energy and wave-bombs and finally stopped in front of three large unmarked crates.

"This one," the guard said and pointed at the middle crate.

Alex pulled out his comm and raised the device to his lips.

"Sheridan to Maglar, we've found the target. Mark my location," he said into the comm.

"Understood. Transport is on its way," Maglar replied in a gruff voice.

"Perfect, Sheridan out," the Ranger said.

He hooked the comm back onto his belt and turned to Cameron.

"Now for the waiting game," Alex said with a smile.

"Sounds like fun—" Cameron stopped midsentence.

"What's wrong?" Alex asked with concern.

Cameron's head whipped from side to side as her eyes darted down the different pathways.

"Cameron, what's wrong?" he asked in a firm tone.

"I can't be sure, but it feels like a—"

As the word Ranger left her lips, Cameron realized she could not hear herself. She looked up at Alex with concern. He also tried to speak but no sound could be heard. He muttered something else. If her lip reading was correct, it was some form of profanity. Alex grabbed ahold of her arm. He ripped Cameron to the ground and activated his fourth ascension.

A bright blue shield erected around them. Cameron could see through the blue tint, but barely. As the barrier rose, a collection of energy bolts pounded against the nearly impregnable shield.

Cameron looked back at the guard. He had drawn his sword and was in a defensive posture.

A second spread of bolts flew over the energy bubble and took out the Turkcanon guard. Her eyes darted back to Alex. He was on one knee with his hand on her shoulder. Cameron peered into his light blue eyes and saw anger. He was still speaking even though she could not hear a word he was saying. Cameron did her best to read his lips and pulled out a slew of profanity.

Another set of bolts pounded against the shield. Alex said something else, but she could not make it out. He shook his head and repeated his last statement. This time slower.

"Hold," she repeated back and tried desperately to understand.

"Hold on!" Cameron exclaimed.

Her eyes opened wide as she realized her mentor was going to do something outside the box.

He grabbed on to her and pulled her small frame close to his body. Another scatter gun blast impacted the barrier. Alex looked beyond the shield. Cameron could tell he was memorizing the location of the attacker. Alex dropped the energy barrier and activated his second ascension. A massive shock wave erupted from his body.

Cameron felt the energy pound against her back. Impacting her person with such force she instantly felt sick and started throwing up. Alex released his grip, stood up and continued firing energy bolts in the direction of their attacker.

Cameron fell to her hands and knees still coughing. She peered up at her mentor who fired energy bursts in different directions.

"Ghosts!" Alex cursed as the area around them was unmuted.

Cameron finally realized who their attacker was. Ranger-Ghosts were the assassins of the Ranger Empire. They not only had stealth but could mute sound in higher ascensions. This made them a truly silent killer.

"Gods I hate that ability," Alex said and continued his rant.

"If we were attacked by a Ranger, why couldn't I fully sense him?" she coughed.

"When a Ghost enters stealth mode it generally scrambles sense and telepathic abilities," Alex explained, "you were lucky to pick him up at all."

Alex pulled his comm off his belt and activated the device.

"Ferrell, we have a big problem," Alex bluntly said into the comm.

"What happened?" Ferrell quickly replied.

"We were just attacked by a Ranger-Ghost."

"Damn it!" Ferrell cursed, "Castus did you hear that?"

"It's not my fault," Castus's voice sounded over the comm.

"I don't accept that. Alex, get the bomb loaded and escort it to the warship," Ferrell commanded.

"Understood James," Alex replied in a calmer tone.

He hooked the comm onto his belt and turned back to Cameron.

"You okay kid?"

"Please don't ever do that again," she replied and continued coughing.

Alex knelt and put his hand on her back.

"Don't worry. That's a last resort move."

Cameron's back hurt while her stomach was in knots. She heard a hum, turned her gaze skyward and saw a Tuskeron transport on its way toward them. Alex extended his arm and helped Cameron to her feet. The black transport coasted down and landed a dozen meters from them. Cameron and Alex made their way over to the ship. As they did the rear hatch opened and a squad of rhino Tuskeron's ran out to secure the area.

"Load that one," Alex commanded and pointed at the correct weapon.

The hybrids made their way forward. The weapon was heavy enough it took all four guards to lift it. They walked in unison and carried the weapon inside the ship. Soon after Alex and Cameron boarded the vessel.

Upon entry, Alex closed and sealed the rear door. The ship lifted off the ground and sped for the Flagship in high orbit.

"Do you think we will be okay?" Cameron asked and turned her gaze to the older Ranger.

Alex stared forward and thought about the question.

"We don't know what he heard. Hopefully he was just after me. Keep your guard up. Who knows what will happen when we get to the rendezvous point," he replied in a cautious tone.

* * *

Almost six hours later, Cameron sat next to Alex and Ferrell in a small shuttle. They had arrived at the Aathis system a short time before and were on one of five dropships bound for the grassy planet below.

Cameron's mind became clouded as the memories of her last encounter with the Draith came flashing back. She was in her room, safe, but terrified. Soon after, she was dragged out like an animal and thrown into a collection of Humans. Cameron was told her life and freedom were gone. That she belonged to someone else and would never be able to make her own choices.

I hate them. If the Draith hadn't attacked Agron, I would still be free, she thought with contempt.

Her mind was ripped back to the present as the shuttle touched down on the planet surface. The hatch lowered and allowed the radiant sunlight into the gloomy dropship. Ferrell stood up first and made his way out of the transport. Cameron and Alex quickly followed and exited the vessel directly behind the black-haired man.

The other transports around them started to unload. There were twelve rhino-bred Tuskeron's. Two of which pushed the hydro-bomb on a hover-lift.

Maglar walked up to Ferrell with his thick mane blowing in the breeze.

"According to sensors, the Draith are over the next ridge," the lion said and pointed to the east.

The rhinos formed up around them, each one holding a Tuskeron assault-rifle and an electrified guards-club.

The group cautiously made their way up the ridge. Once they made it to the summit, Cameron gazed down the hill and saw the black armor of the Hunters. The Draith had arrived ahead and setup a base camp. They had taken position a hundred meters or so away from their fearsome Darkwings, which sat in the tall grass.

The Ninth Faction group moved down the hill and stopped a half dozen meters from their quarry. There were twelve Hunters around the edges, each one holding a bladed staff weapon. In the center of the group stood three additional Draith. They were dressed in silver body armor, signifying their rank as Hunt Master. Cameron noticed an insignia on the top right side of their chest plates. Each one unique and of its own design. This meant they were Clan Leaders and sat at the top of the Draith military.

Ferrell and Maglar advanced with Cameron and Alex right behind them. Two of the Clan Leaders stepped forward while the third took position in the back with the Hunters.

Cameron's eyes drifted past the ranking Clan Leader to a medium sized animal approach. It was a Draith hound. Six legs, floppy ears with thick mangy hair. The creature had long hooked fangs that were meant for gripping and holding their prey. The hound sauntered forward and stood next to his master.

"Saal'li'Mar, first son of Kar'Raa'desh, Clan Leader and Hunt Master of the combined Draith fleet," Ferrell said and greeted the lead Draith by his full title.

This greeting was customary when speaking to a Draith.

"James Ferrell, Slave Lord, ruler of Camus and ranking member of the Ninth Faction council," Saal'li'Mar replied.

"No'Vaa, fourth son of Kar'Raa'desh, Clan Leader and Hunt Master of Cannton," Maglar said and repeated the process.

"Maglar, born of Condor Pride, ruler of Tawson-Four, member of the Ninth Faction council and Commander of the Tuskeron fleet," No'Vaa said and finished the lengthy introductions.

"So on to the negotiations. The Ninth Faction will give you a planet-class hydro-bomb to be used against the Ranger Empire. In exchange we want a non-aggression treaty against Ninth-Faction vessels, two hundred Human slaves, one hundred Accaren slaves, and the Draith clans guarantee they will stay out of Human Republic space after the Rangers have been defeated," Ferrell said addressing their steep terms.

No'Vaa's gaze turned to his brother and then back to the Slave Lord.

"Unacceptable," No'Vaa interjected, "the Draith clans will begin our invasion into the Human Republic after we've exterminated the filth of the Rangers."

Saal'li'Mar raised his hand and silenced his younger brother.

"Our counter proposal," Saal'li'Mar said in a gruff yet methodical voice, "we split the territories. The Ninth Faction would have: Araka, Geneva, Kemish, Jasna, Ragnar, Lyari and the rest of the core worlds. The Draith will take Brighton, Cal'lia, and Vera-5."

No'Vaa turned once again at the generous offer.

"What of Agron and Quinn?" Maglar asked.

"Neutral planets," the lead Draith said.

No'Vaa hissed to himself at the response.

Ferrell glanced over at Maglar who nodded in agreement.

"I have to ask, Saal'li'Mar, what's in it for the Draith? Other than two and a half military bases the Draith clans gain little from this," Ferrell questioned.

Saal'li'Mar took a step forward. Ferrell matched his stance and stood toe to toe with the eldest son of Kar'Raa'desh. The Draith towered over the Slave Lord, but Ferrell held his pose and cranked his head skyward.

"The Ninth Faction will never conquer or destroy the Human Republic," Saal'li'Mar sneered confidently, "you will only take them as a work force."

Ferrell's face lit up with a sly smile at the Draith's explanation.

"Chief Kar'Raa'desh wants the Slave Lords returning to true power," Saal'li'Mar finished.

"The Ninth Faction accepts your offer, Saal'li'Mar first son of Kar'Raa'desh," Ferrell replied.

"Agreed James Ferrell," the Draith stated.

He turned back and joined his brother.

"Where are the access codes for the hydro-bomb?" the lead Draith demanded.

Ferrell turned back and motioned to Alex. The Energy-Caster stepped forward and pulled a data pad out of his rear pocket. As he approached the Clan Leader, the Draith hound snarled and snapped its jaws at the Ranger with hostile intent. Saal'li'Mar instantly raised and aimed his tri-shot battle-rifle at Alex.

The Ranger raised his hands in defense, blue energy swirling around them. A split second later, guards on both sides lifted their weapons. Cameron raised her hands in defense and was ready for the command to attack.

"Stop!" Ferrell commanded.

"My hound is trained to hunt and detect Rangers," Saal'li'Mar snarled.

"Why do you have a Ranger with you Slave Lord?" No'Vaa yelled in absolute hatred at the Rangers presence.

"Alex Sheridan, fifth ascension Energy-Caster, head of Camus security, personal bodyguard and enforcer for James Ferrell," the Ranger replied, following the customs to the Draith's surprise.

"Former Ranger Infiltrator Alex Sheridan?" the third Clan Leader interjected.

"Be silent Rift, Seventh Son," No'Vaa yelled back and did not take the time to repeat his full title.

"Garron, speaks highly of you in his slave trades and other dealings," Rift continued and ignored his brother.

Garron was a Tuskeron Warlord and the ruler of Vau'Tir. He controlled one of four main defense points along the border of the Ninth Faction and Human Republic.

"We don't need to fight," Ferrell interjected.

Alex stretched forth his hand and extended the data pad toward Saal'li'Mar. The hound growled as the Clan Leader reached forward and took hold of the pad. The Energy-Caster turned and walked back to the rest of his party. Both sides still had their weapons raised prepared to strike at any point.

Ferrell motioned for the guards to bring the hydro-bomb. The Tuskerons pushed the hover pad forward and released control to the awaiting Hunters.

"Are we good?" Ferrell asked sharply.

"For now. Keep in mind Slave Lord, once we are done exterminating what is left of the Ranger's we will revisit our talks regarding the Human worlds—"

Before he could finish his statement, lightning bolts struck the ground around them and took out Draith and Tuskeron alike.

"Rangers!" Alex yelled and pointed to a Lightning-Caster standing about seventy meters from them. Two other Rangers stood beside the caster. The second enhanced being took to flight and appeared to be a Ranger-Hawk. The Ranger flew around the outer edges of the group firing a myriad of energy missiles, energy bombs and beams from his eyes. The aerial assault burned three of the guards around Cameron while the bombs took out another two. The surviving Tuskeron's returned fire, but the Ranger-Hawk swooped to the left and moved out of range.

The Draith opened fire on the third Ranger who sprinted toward them at top speed. Cameron focused on the bright flashes and saw the bolts pound into the female Ranger's barrier. She was a Shield-Tech and like all her breed was fearless in her assault. She charged forward and struck the first Hunter with a shielded-punch. The hit launched the two-and-a-half-meter alien off the ground and into the air. After a moment, the creature landed and rolled up to Cameron. She gazed down at the wounded Draith and saw the front of his breastplate had been warped by the hit.

"Secure the weapon!" Saal'li'Mar commanded to his Hunters.

Saal'li'Mar turned back to his hound and spoke in his native language. Cameron was not sure what he said, but the hound howled and stood in a defensive posture next to Cameron. Saal'li'Mar and No'Vaa exchanged glances and sprinted toward the attacking Shield-Tech.

"Take down the Hawk," Cameron heard Alex command from her left, "I'll deal with the caster."

She turned to see her mentor take off toward the hill with a clutch of Tuskeron's at his back. Alex activated his third ascension and created a solid wall of energy. The Lightning-Caster fired a variety of bolts which absorbed into his shield, but Alex kept the barrier moving forward and closed the gap between them.

Cameron turned her focus back to his orders and peered skyward. The Hawk had looped back around and was prepared for his next attack run. The Ranger swooped and weaved back and forth as he seemed to stay one step ahead of his ground kept targets.

A blue ball of energy formed around the Ranger's chest as he moved into position. His line of attack was clear.

"The hydro-bomb," Cameron whispered out loud.

The Ranger-Telekinetic lashed out with her mind, took hold of the Hawk and threw him toward the grassy planes. Caught off guard, the Hawk lost control of his ability and fired the energy bomb a half dozen meters in front of Cameron before he crashed into the grass.

A second later, the bomb exploded taking out a Draith Hunter and a Tuskeron. The fire roared up and Cameron was thrown to the ground from the force of the shockwave.

She quickly recovered and raised her hands in defense, palms outward. Her breaths were rapid while her heart pounded. As the young Ranger peered for her quarry, her stomach turned to knots. All the sound from the battle had vanished.

"I despise Ghosts!" she yelled silently and took on her mentor's crass view on the ability.

Out of the corner of her eye Cameron saw the hound leap toward her. Cameron gasped and feared the dog like creature meant her harm, but the hound continued and brushed by her as he passed.

Cameron whipped around and saw the creature attack the ground. Soon the image became clear. The hound sunk his long fangs into the Ranger-Ghost. The male Ranger became visible and yelled out in pain. The sound of the battle returned with full strength. It was so overwhelming Cameron was forced to cover her ears as she fell to her knees.

The hound shook its head back and forth putting the Ghost in even more pain. Cameron could see the blood covered fangs pierced the Ranger's calve. The hound dug in with all six legs, drug the brutalized Ranger back to the Darkwing and left a trail of blood as it went.

Cameron made it back to her feet and turned her attention back to the Ranger-Hawk. She scanned the landscape and after a few passes she finally saw him. The Ranger-Hawk was still recovering and had just made it to his feet.

The Hawk took to flight, but Cameron was ready for him. She grabbed ahold of the Ranger with her abilities and with one fluid motion slammed the Hawk back into the ground.

The Ranger made a rapid recovery. He rolled to one knee and powered up his first ascension. With his gaze focused on Cameron, his eyes lit up with orange intensity as two energy beams shot out. They hit with perfect accuracy and impacted the upper left side of Cameron's chest and shoulder.

Cameron screamed out in pain and fell backwards. She hit the ground with a thud. Cameron's head was spinning, and she could feel the deep burns caused by her adversary. She tried to sit up, but the pain in her chest and shoulder made it unbearable.

Cameron gasped as a bright silver boot stomped into the grass beside her head. Her eye's flashed skyward to see Rift, Clan Leader and Seventh son of Kar'Raa'desh. His weapon was flush with his shoulder and his eyes fixed ahead on his target.

Cameron's eyes fell past the alien. She saw the Ranger-Hawk and powered up his first ascension. Just as before two orange beams shot forth and hit Rift directly in the chest.

The Draith braced himself and took the attack head on. He pulled the trigger and fired three bolts from his tri-shot battle-rifle. The yellow bolts sped forward and clipped the Ranger on his left leg and rib cage.

The Hawk lost control of his ability and plummeted to the earth. Rift swapped to his missile launcher with the click of a button. The Seventh Son aimed and with perfect accuracy fired a missile into the ground beneath the falling Ranger. A loud explosion sounded, and flames erupted burning the grass. The Hawk was caught in the blaze and died on impact.

Rift lowered his weapon and turned his silver eyed gaze down on Cameron. She was not sure what to think and nervously readjusted her hood.

After a moment, Rift reached down and extended his hand to the Ranger-Telekinetic. She accepted the help and took hold with her right hand. The Draith effortlessly helped the teenager to her feet and without another word moved to help his brothers.

Cameron was still in awe at the Draith's almost kind gesture. It was the first time she had ever witness any action like it. She gave a solid shake of her head, shrugged off the pain and observed the progress of the battlefield.

Three quarters of the Tuskerons and over half the Draith were dead. Their bodies spread across the grasslands. Cameron caught sight of Alex who sprinted back toward her. She looked past her mentor but saw no sign of the Lightning-Caster.

Hearing screaming, Cameron turned back to the Darkwing. She saw Saal'li'Mar dragging the wounded Ranger Shield-Tech. She kicked and fought but did not have the strength to raise her barrier. After a few steps, the famed Clan Leader stopped and beat his prey into submission. The screams turned into bone chilling cries for help as Saal'li'Mar drug her inside the lead Darkwing.

Cameron stood in shock of what she had witnessed. She knew the exact fate the female Ranger had been damned too.

"Gods, let her die fast," Cameron whispered mournfully, but deep down she knew it was too much to hope for.

"Come on kid," Alex yelled and ripped her attention back to the present, "we need to go. Now!"

Cameron ran after him and gripped her burned chest as she went. The remaining taskforce made it back to the dropships. Cameron took her customary seat next to her mentor, buckled her belt and examined her injuries.

"Are you alright?" he asked,

"The Hawk tagged me," Cameron replied with a frown.

"Here," Alex said in a dry tone and handed her a small container of AHC.

Cameron took off the lid and started applying it on the burn. Her eyes caught sight of Alex who leaned forward. His arms rested on his legs and his gaze stayed fixed on the grated floor.

"Are you alright?" she asked.

"I'm just fine, Cammy," he replied with a fake smile.

Cameron new him well enough to know when he was not being one hundred percent honest. She decided to drop the subject, leaned back in her chair and counted down the minutes until they were home safe on Camus.

* * *

Two days had passed after Cameron's horrific experience on Aathis, and each night her mind faced the same nightmare. The gut churning screams from the female Shield-Tech. Her cries for help, and the knowledge of what her fate would be.

Torture and death, Cameron thought with sadness.

She sat on the edge of her bed. Hands covered her face with her knees pulled up to her chest.

She had been granted a break from her everyday routine to allow her wounds from the Ranger-Hawk to heal.

Cameron wore a sport bra with white bandages wrapped over her chest in multiple places. She had bootcut jeans, a thick leather belt and was barefoot. Cameron uncovered her face and gazed toward the balcony.

It was getting late and the sun had already dipped beyond the horizon. The breeze was cool, and the air smelled of flowers which hung from the edges of the railing.

Cameron heard a loud, sharp knock at the entrance to her quarters. Surprised, she quickly stood up, put on a form fitting robe and answered the door. Shock filled her expressions as she gazed upon James Ferrell. He was dressed in a charcoal grey suit, polished dress shoes and was holding a glass of Scotch.

"Good evening, Cameron," he said in a deep voice.

His tone was unusually polite and put her on edge. She froze for the briefest of moments while pondering the question at hand.

Gods why is he at my quarters, Cameron panicked.

In all the time she had spent on Camus, this was the first Ferrell had visited her without Alex and was the second time he had ever been to her room.

"May I come in?" he asked and brought Cameron out of her trance.

Yes sir," Cameron quickly replied.

She stepped to the side and allowed Ferrell to enter her room. He stood for a moment and observed her decorations.

"I like the painting," he said and pointed at the Accaren artwork Alex had picked up for her a few months before.

"Is something wrong?" Cameron tentatively asked in a quiet tone.

"Oh no, Cameron," Ferrell said with a devious smile, "I wanted to give this to you personally."

He pulled a small holo-pad out of his pocket and handed it to the young Ranger.

"Today is a day which will be celebrated for a thousand years," Ferrell proclaimed, "it's not public knowledge yet but two hours ago the Draith began their assault on Rydon. Thirty minutes ago, the Draith launched a hydro-bomb into the planets core and killed all its inhabitants. Six point three billion dead."

The news hit Cameron like a ten-ton weight. It was the memory of the Shield-Tech times the dead count. Although she had limited contact with her people, she was still a Ranger and had a hand in their demise.

"Thank you for helping me put you're people on the endangered species list," Ferrell said to Cameron's repulsion.

Ferrell seemed happy. This only added to the brown eyed Ranger's fury. Cameron did her best but failed to hide her facial expressions, but Ferrell did not care and continued smiling. She could tell the pain gave him pleasure.

"Does Alex know?" she asked and tried to contain her emotions.

"He was in the tactical center when I received the report," Ferrell replied.

Cameron stood in silence and stared at the holo-pad.

"Goodnight, Cameron" Ferrell said and broke the silence.

He walked forward and kissed her on the head. She wanted to run but held her ground and refused to flinch.

"Tomorrow is a new day, a day without the ignorance and hypocrisy that was the Ranger Empire," Ferrell sneered as he shut the door.

Cameron turned on the recording. It was a holo-video of five Darkwings. They split away from the main attack fleet. The ships whipped and dodged through the Ranger lines. Passing over an ARC-class heavy cruiser, the beams on the ship cut down two of the Darkwings. They flew forward and launched the weapon down into the planet.

Cameron teared up as she watched the planet change color and become white in a matter of minutes. She turned off the recording and threw it across the room. The device shattered upon hitting the adjacent wall. Cameron turned and ran out of her room. She sprinted as fast as she could to Alex's chambers. The fourteen-year-old skidded to a stop and knocked on the Energy-Casters door.

"I said I didn't want to be disturbed," Alex's voice sounded through the thick wood.

"Alex, it's me. I need to talk with you," Cameron pleaded, nearly at the point of tears.

"Come in, Cammy," he said after a second.

Cameron slowly opened the door and looked in. Alex sat on the ground with his back pressed against the wall with his eyes fixed on his bed. There was a bottle of whisky on the floor next to him. He held a crystalline glass that was half empty. For the first time Cameron saw her mentor truly drunk. She shut the door and walked over to him.

"Take a seat, Cammy Lynn," he said and laughed to himself.

Cameron sat legs crossed and faced Alex with her back to the bed.

He picked up the bottle and refilled his glass. The gurgle of the alcohol pouring into his glass was the only sound that could be heard. He set the bottle next to him and took a large swill.

"So, if I had to guess, Ferrell told you, didn't he?" Alex asked.

"He gave me a holo-video of the ending battle," she replied with a sniffle, "he gloated Alex! He thanked me for helping to bring an end to our people!"

Cameron finally broke down. She put her hands over her face as tears poured from her eyes.

"Sorry Cammy," Alex replied in an empathetic tone, "I'm sure James made some comment about the end of the Ranger Empire."

"Yeah, he did," Cameron responded and brought her tears to a standstill.

"Dick," Alex cursed and handed Cameron the glass of alcohol, "you need this more than I do."

"Are you going to be alright?" Cameron asked.

She took her first sip of the bitter alcohol and gave out a slight cough.

"Good girl," he said with a smile.

Cameron returned his expression and took another sip of whisky.

"What happens now?" she asked.

"We are part of a dying race, Cameron. Welcome to the damned," he replied and raised the bottle.

RAID ON ARAKA

It had been just over two years since the fall of Rydon and in that time Known-Space had changed drastically. A month after the tragedy, the united Draith Clans broke into a civil war. No'Vaa's fleet attacked So'Lar the third son of Kar'Raa'desh. The Draith broke off their alliance and fighting filled their ranks once again.

This was perfect for the Ninth Faction.

"Looks like we won't have to renegotiate for the Human worlds," Ferrell said after the fractioning of the Clans.

On the other side of the coin, this meant they would not have the advantage of the Human Republic fighting a two-front war. The Ninth Faction was forced to wait until the time was right, but that day had finally come.

Cameron stood at the sink in her room and gazed at her reflection in the mirror. It had taken a while, but she had started to finally accept her role in Ferrell's organization. The Tuskeron's on Camus revered the Telekinetic's skill and respected her as Ferrell's newest lieutenant.

Alex and Cameron had been on dozens of smaller raids. They would either attack the outer Human worlds such as Quinn and Agron, or harder targets such as Jasna or Iceler. They traveled along the border of Ninth Faction space raiding ships and small convoys.

On a personal note, Alex and Cameron had just returned from Syprus. She had turned sixteen only a few days before. As a present to the brown-haired Ranger, Alex booked one night at a small casino for them. They each had a well-kept room and enjoyed the amenities of the luxurious gaming club.

The time had come to unite the Slave Lords. For the first time in seven years the most powerful and hated Humans in Known-Space would be in the same room.

Cameron walked over to her closet and pulled her new black leather coat off the hanger. Like her shroud it covered her face with holo emitters. Cameron loved the feel of the silk interior. It buttoned up in front and had a belt which wrapped tightly around her waist.

She put on the coat, fastened it and pulled up the hood. Cameron put on her combat boots and laced them up. She was ready.

At least I hope so, Cameron thought with a crooked smile.

Cameron exited her room and shut the door firmly. She sauntered down the hallway and checked the finer details of her appearance as she went. She made her way to the powerlift and took the three-level journey to the throne room. Cameron exited the powerlift, turned the final corner and approached the double doors.

Both Tuskeron guards took hold and swiftly opened the doors for their lieutenant. Cameron walked down the small set of stairs and noticed the group off to the right. They were standing around a circular holo-map.

Behind the device was a long range comm-unit with a Narairian on it. The insect stood impatiently as its jaw snapped.

Cameron walked over and stood next to Alex in the back. The teen Ranger took a moment and peered over the room. To the right stood Alexandria Morgan, ancestor to the legendary Old Earth bounty hunter family. She was in her mid-thirties, tanned skin with thick black hair. The Morgan's, although depleted in numbers were still feared for their training, armor, and family loyalty.

Alexandria on the other hand had chosen to broaden her family legacy. As a young bounty hunter, she quickly moved to the top and turned to slave trading. A few years later, she was granted the rank as the first female Slave Lord and trading rights in fifty percent of the old Accaren Empire.

Aden Stark stood next to her. He had a short, average build and stood in contrast to the beautiful Human woman. Aden did ninety percent of his dealings in Unexplored-Space which was located opposite of the Void. He had strong ties to the Narairian Hive and races beyond the Known.

Behind them were two lion-bred Tuskeron's she recognized instantly. The first was Maglar who Cameron had met once before. The second was Garron who was the Warlord of Vau'Tir. Their orange manes were full, and their eyes filled with intensity.

A sickened look swept over Cameron's face as she saw Conrad Masters who stood opposite Alexandria. The twenty-two-year-old Slave Lord had the same scrawny build she remembered. Conrad had taken control of his father's slave empire after Reid Masters died mysteriously.

The rumor was Conrad had either killed him or had paid someone to do the nefarious deed for him. Cameron had met him once before on her first trip to the bazaar.

He referred to me as a parafek and slapped my ass, Cameron remembered, still angered by the encounter, *I thought Alex was going to kill him.*

Beside him stood Colin Trails. He was a tall, strong man who stood ten centimeters above Alex. He had a thick black beard with eyes that held a dark and menacing stare at the holographic map before him.

Colin Trails and his brother Casen Trails started originally in the weapons industry. From there Colin branched off into slave trading. His brother Casen Trails stayed with the weapons, and together the Trails brothers shared control of the old Accaren Empire with Alexandria.

In a matter of eight years, Colin had ascended nearly to the top of the food chain and had slave ships in over half of Known-Space. He stood second only to Ferrell in slaves, money and territory. Colin had close ties to many Accaren tribes and would deal in Accaren slaves. He also captured Valari and sold them to fight in arenas around the Ninth Faction.

He's a mean, brutal son of a bitch, Cameron remembered Alex saying.

Before his rise to power, Colin was wanted by the Human Republic and the Ranger Empire on crimes ranging but not limited to: Human trafficking, marketing of illegal weapons, forty-five counts of assault, fifty-four accounts of battery, twenty-five counts of murder and twenty-eight accounts of rape.

His bodyguard, Damarious Ta'ag stood beside him. He was an Accaren warrior who spoke for the mighty Ta'ag tribe. One of the strongest in the old Accaren Empire. He wore native blue Accaren Knight armor, with his helmet tucked neatly under his arm.

The Accaren had tanned skin, a powerful build, with two blue octagon tattoos. One located under each eye. There was an Accaren hand-cannon strapped to his right leg with an Accaren short sword on the left.

Ferrell stood in front of them, his black hair pulled back in a ponytail and wore a charcoal grey suit with matching shoes.

"Today my fellow Slave Lords, is a special day. This is the opportunity we've been waiting for," Ferrell proclaimed in a deep and powerful voice.

Ferrell pulled a small remote out of his jacket pocket. He pressed the center button and changed to the next series of images on the holo-map. The map shifted and after a second a planet appeared.

"This is Araka. Human controlled and on the border of Republic and Ninth Faction Space. Our target," he stated.

"How do you expect to attack a Human planet on the edge of the core systems? Reinforcements will be dispatched from Geneva or Ragnar," Alexandria questioned in a blunt tone.

"Since the fall of the Ranger Empire, the Human Republic has been slowly losing ground over the past year. They don't have the ships to fight all of us," Ferrell replied with a dark smile.

"But that doesn't mean this will be a successful venture," Alexandria retorted.

Ferrell paced back and forth upon hearing the statement.

"That's why we're going to have some help," he replied and turned back to the holo-screen with the Narairian on it.

"At this point we have fifteen Narairian strikers and ten cruisers standing by on the border of Human space. Their job is to engage the fleet over Geneva. The Republic will pull ships from Araka to counter, this is our window for a planet wide assault," Ferrell proposed.

The group contemplated his daring plan.

"You will each be assigned one of the major cities to raid. Our goal is to round up as many Humans as we can and retreat before their fleet can make the jump back. Maglar and Garron will be our taskforce and have a total of forty Tuskeron warships," Ferrell proclaimed.

"Bold plan, Ferrell," Aden commented, "I like it."

"Prepare your forces. We leave within the hour," the ranking Slave Lord commanded.

Without another word the other Slave Lords exited the throne room. This left Ferrell, Alex and Cameron standing next to the holo-map.

"Well that went well," Alex commented.

"Better than the last time," Ferrell replied.

"So, what's our plan of attack?" Cameron asked and stared intently at the holo-map.

"Our attack force will be split into two teams. Alex, you and your team will be landing here," Ferrell said and pointed to a medium sized city on the northern hemisphere.

"Understood," Alex replied.

"Cameron, you and your team will be landing a few hundred kilometers north of Alex's location," Ferrell said and turned to the teen Ranger.

Her heart skipped a beat as the words left his mouth. For the past three years Cameron had trained with Alex and had acted as his lieutenant. This was the first time she would have her own assault force, her own command.

"What are my objectives?" Cameron asked.

"Your goal is simple. Lead as many men, women and children on to the slave barges as fast as you can. We may only have a few hours until the Humans can counter," Ferrell explained.

"Understood sir," Cameron replied with a nod of her shrouded head.

"I'll be assigning Sargus to your team, Cameron," Alex said and referred to the lead Tuskeron guard who the Telekinetic had worked with over the years.

"Get to your ships. We have a world to enslave," Ferrell said with a sly smile.

Cameron glared over at the Slave Lord, her leather hood covering most of her expressions. It was a look she had used more than once in recent years at the vile nature of his breed. Cameron turned and walked with Alex behind the throne and into the powerlift.

"Are you nervous?" he asked as they started their ascent.

Cameron peered up at him with a puzzled gaze.

"Your first command?" Alex commented.

Although he could not see her face, Alex knew the young Telekinetic well enough to read her body language.

"A bit," Cameron replied honestly.

"In the Ranger military, this would have been your first step in becoming an Infiltrator or Infantry Commander," Alex said and reminded Cameron of the possible future stolen from her.

"I would be promoted in the Ranger military?" she questioned, "I mean with what Simon Cail did."

"Your telekinetic gifts are impressive, but your Sense ability is what the Empire would have used. You would have made the perfect Captain, a Ranger Infiltrator as I was," Alex said with pride.

He reached behind his jacket and pulled out a small holstered energy-pistol. It was a custom weapon, blackened coloring with a form-fitting grip.

"You're going to need this," Alex said and handed her the compact weapon.

Cameron inspected the weapon and notice it had a stun setting for incapacitating targets.

"Thank you," Cameron replied and strapped the weapon to her belt.

"Just remember, never rely on your abilities, keep your eyes open, and be safe," Alex said and put his hand on her back.

The powerlift doors opened, and the pair walked to their separate dropships.

"Good luck, Cammy," Alex yelled over to her.

"Don't get into too much trouble without me," she replied with a crooked smile.

Cameron entered the transport. Soon after, the vessel took off and headed to the fleet above.

* * *

A matter of hours later, Cameron stood in the middle of the hanger bay. She had just been informed they were approaching the planet and was prepared to board one of the many dropships in the bay. Cameron turned her gaze to the large shielded door. Blue rings passed by the hanger as the ship continued through subspace.

Sargus stood beside her, he wore leather Tuskeron armor with an assault-rifle slung over his shoulder. The rhino had two holsters, one on each hip. The first held a Tuskeron beam-cannon. A weapon meant for stunning targets with a powerful beam. The second housed an electrified guards club.

Cameron turned her attention back to the hanger bay and observed the hundreds of Tuskeron's around her. They each had their own task. Either loading equipment or boarding a transport.

Deeper in the hanger bay, Cameron saw the massive slave barges each identical in design and could hold up to two hundred slaves a peace. Cameron looked over to her right and saw a large crate. She walked forward and climbed on top of it. This put her just above the Tuskeron's eye level.

"Can you get their attention please?" Cameron asked Sargus in a polite tone.

"Listen up!" Sargus roared at the top of his lungs.

The hybrids voice echoed through the hanger bay. After a second the other Tuskerons turned their gaze to the sixteen-year-old Ranger. Cameron stood in silence for a moment and nervously readjusted her leather hood.

"I just received word we are approaching the Araka system. We know why we're here, let's get the job done!" she yelled out and ignited the passion of her battalion.

Roars sounded from the other hybrids as they moved to board their ships.

Cameron hopped off her perch and made her way toward one of the dropships with Sargus close behind. They walked up to the lead dropship and entered through the side door of the vessel. Cameron slipped behind the pilot and took a seat in one of the Human sized chairs. Sargus lumbered past her and took a seat in the middle next to the other five Tuskeron's. Each one hooked on to a rappel line secured above their head.

Cameron pulled out a small data-pad which sat beside her. She activated the device and external sensor readings appeared. There were over forty Tuskeron warships traveling through subspace in formation.

The dropship shook as the fleet exited subspace. The map readjusted and displayed a single planet system with ten Human frigates defending it. Twenty of the warships broke off and engaged the Human fleet. Cameron watched the screen in amazement as the horde of Tuskeron warships overtook the Human vessels one by one. Although the Human frigates were larger, the Tuskerons concentrated their fire and destroyed the ships in sets of two.

The dropship shook again as it lifted off the hanger bay floor and flew out. Cameron looked back at her sensors and saw over three hundred dropships all bound for different parts of the planet. The barges lifted off next and followed the smaller ships down.

"One minute to drop," the pilot yelled back.

Cameron put away her data-pad and prepared her mind for battle. The vessel came to a holt and the overhead lights turned green.

"Jump time, grunts," the Tuskeron pilot yelled back.

The chairs underneath the Tuskeron's dropped out and the rhinos fell from sight. The rappel lines squealed as they absorbed the weight of the behemoths.

"You ready, lieutenant?" the pilot asked.

"Let's do this," she replied in a confident tone.

Cameron took a deep breath and a second later her chair dropped out. Without a rappel harness Cameron rapidly fell to the ground below. She moved her hands to her sides, activated her ascension and slowed her descent. Cameron's combat boots hit the ground with a thud. She raised her hands in defense and took a moment to observe the small logging town.

Horrified screams and weapons fire filled the air as the streets filled with chaos. Cameron watched two of her troops kick in a door, fire their beam weapons inside and enter the small dwelling. Seconds later the guards returned and pulled a mother and daughter into the street by their hair. Dozens of Humans bolted from their homes and tried to make a desperate escape to the north.

Cameron drew her pistol. She changed the firing mode to stun and with perfect accuracy shot two Humans sprinting for a back alleyway. Soon after, a rhino-bred Tuskeron walked forward, grabbed the Humans by the leg and drug them back to the awaiting slave barge.

Three Human guards ran out from behind a nearby building. They wore light armor, and each had a standard HT-52 combat rifle. Sargus opened fire with his beam cannon and hit two of the guards. Cameron grabbed the final guard with her abilities and fired two stun bolts into his chest. The Human shook for a moment before consciousness left him. She released her grip and allowed the soldier to fall to the ground.

Wails and screams for help sounded from every corner of the city. Cameron's division systematically moved like a wave through the settlement. Starting from the south, they ended up at the far north end. The Humans fought back trying desperately to draw a line in the sand, but each time the massive hybrids blitzed their way through and took even more slaves.

In a far shorter time then Cameron had expected, they pushed the Humans back to their final stand. They had created a makeshift wall on the border of the northern forest. Cameron, Sargus and the rest of the Tuskeron's took shelter behind the final row of houses. Dozens of energy bolts flew between both sides and made it impossible to gain a clear shot. The few remaining Human civilians fled past the makeshift wall and into the thick woods behind. More than one innocent Human was gunned down in a desperate attempt to make it to safety.

As the firefight raged on, Cameron's mind became clouded. She could feel the aura of a more powerful being.

"We have another Ranger in play," Cameron said to the rest of her team.

She whipped out her comm and held it to her chapped lips.

"What's our ETA on loading the slaves?" Cameron asked in a blunt tone.

"We are seventy-five percent completed," a Tuskeron's voice sounded after a moment.

"Alright, move as fast as you can, we might have to get out of here in a hurry," Cameron replied and hooked her comm back to her leather belt.

A blur streaked behind the Human line, and after a moment they ceased fire. Cameron held up her hand and commanded her troops to do the same. For the first time since they had landed silence filled the air.

"Slaver scum, you are trespassing in Human Republic space. Return the Humans you have taken illegally, and we will let you leave with your heads still attached to your bodies," the Ranger threatened from behind the Human line.

"That's not going to happen. We already have them loaded. Do you really want to sacrifice more Human lives?" Cameron yelled back.

She matched the Ranger's tone and tried to bluff her way out. Cameron pressed her back against the building as the Humans opened fire on their location. Without a command given, the Tuskerons around her returned fire. The deafening sound of their assault-rifles echoed through the alleyway. Cameron fired two energy bolts around the corner of the building, but quickly pulled back and avoided the Human's counterattack. Woodchips splattered against her face as the energy bolts nearly hit their mark.

A blur sped in front of her. Before Cameron could react, she felt her body being lifted off the ground. The Speedster continued her momentum and carried the Telekinetic away from the battlefield. Cameron came to a sudden stop as she felt her back slam into the wall of a small building. With her head spinning, and blurred vision Cameron gazed over her attacker. She was petite, athletic build, with short brown hair and hazel eyes. The Ranger was younger than Cameron had expected and was near to her own age. The Speedster's eyes filled with hatred as they stayed locked on her.

Cameron grabbed the Speedster's wrist and twisted it to the side, the Ranger teen was forced to release her grip on the Telekinetic. Cameron followed up with a left cross and struck her across the face. Losing her balance, the Speedster fell to the ground. The Telekinetic stepped forward to kick her, but before she could the Speedster shifted her ability into high gear and blurred forward.

The Ranger-Speedster assaulted Cameron with five different lightning fast strikes. The Telekinetic could not see them coming and was hit by each one. The Speedster landed hits to Cameron's right inner thigh and on the left side of her rib cage. With one fluid motion she lifted her target off the ground. Cameron felt herself moving backward and a second later crashed through the door of the single-family home.

They wrestled on the wooden floor for control. Gaining the upper hand, the Speedster knelt on top of Cameron and started swinging. The young Telekinetic took three hits before she could even raise her hands in defense. Cameron took hold of the Speedster with her ascension and threw her back into one of the small bedrooms. Cameron rolled to her feet and raised her bloodied fists.

The opposing Ranger quickly recovered and blurred toward the Telekinetic. Cameron tracked the Speedster's trajectory to the best of her ability and calculated where she would end up. The Telekinetic lowered her center of gravity and braced herself for the incoming assault.

The Speedster came to a stop and swung with a right hook. Cameron ducked under the incoming attack and tackled the teenager. She lifted her by the legs and threw them both into the bedroom. They rolled across the floor and this time Cameron ended up on top. She threw punch after punch at the thinly built Ranger.

The Speedster lifted her leg and pressed her calf against Cameron's neck. With one motion, she ripped the Telekinetic back and threw her to the floor. The Speedster climbed on top and mounted the Telekinetic once again. Cameron covered her face and tried to minimize the damage she was taking.

In the briefest of moments Cameron saw a nightstand off to the side of the bed. She stretched out her hand and exposed her right side to attack.

The opposing Ranger took full advantage of this and landed two solid hits.

Cameron used what remaining strength she had and hurled the piece of furniture at the Speedster.

The solid wood object flew with miraculous velocity and collided with the opposing Ranger. It slammed into her shoulder and whipped her head to the side. Blood sprayed across Cameron's face and coat as the Speedster's body slumped forward. She fell onto Cameron with her lifeless head resting on the Telekinetic's shoulder.

Cameron could feel the Ranger's blood drip down her neck and soak into her shirt. She franticly pushed the body off her and scooted back against the wall.

Cameron peered into the teen's cold dead eyes. They were still open with her unresponsive gaze fixed on the Telekinetic. Cameron was out of breath and her head was spinning. She looked at her hands, knuckles split open and covered in blood.

"Gods!" Cameron screamed in mournful agony at her actions.

She took off her hood and wiped her face, but the blood only seemed to smear. The Telekinetic quickly pulled up her hood upon sensing another being in the room. Her head whipped to the right with her hands raised in defense.

To the back of the room was a small bed, table and a dresser. As she observed closer, Cameron saw a little girl hiding under the bed. She had long brown hair and big brown eyes. From Cameron's estimation she was twelve or thirteen, the same age she was when Ferrell made her a slave. The girl was terrified. She huddled back against the wall holding a small red-haired doll. Cameron struggled to her feet and limped over to the bed. She knelt and looked at the girls tear stained eyes.

"Don't touch me!" the Human child cried out defensively.

"Shh..." Cameron said and put her finger to her lips which silenced the girl.

The Telekinetic knew her assignment, and what Ferrell expected of her. They expected her to do her job and enslave the child.

Could this be a kindness? Cameron thought, *who knows where her parents or family are. They could already be on one of the barges.*

The thought process made Cameron sick. In that moment, she realized the depths she had fallen in her own lack of morality.

"Stay silent and do not leave until help arrives," Cameron said quietly to the girl.

"Cameron," Sargus's voice sounded over the Ranger's comm.

Cameron stood up and pulled the device off her belt.

"I'm here," she replied.

"The Humans are in full retreat and we are heading back to the transports. What's your location?"

"In the center of town," Cameron replied.

She made her way out of the small house and gave one final glance at the girl before exiting.

"I'm on my way back to the drop zone," she replied and hooked the comm back to her belt.

Cameron walked through the barren streets and soon came to the dropships. She made her way over to Sargus who waited for her. The rhino looked over and noticed the Telekinetic was covered in blood.

"What happened?" he asked gruffly.

"I had an encounter with a Ranger-Speedster," Cameron said in an emotionless tone.

"Well done," Sargus grunted and walked onto the transport.

Cameron gave one final look toward the slave barges. They were taking off one by one, heading for the space above. She knew each one was full of innocent Humans she had helped enslave.

"Cameron, warships are detecting a Human fleet in orbit. It's time to go," Sargus's voice sounded from inside the dropship.

Cameron whipped around and took her seat. Seconds later, the hatch shut, and the ship lifted off. It followed the rest of the dropships back to the awaiting warships above Araka. The vessel shook as it landed. The hatch opened, and Cameron made her way out onto the deck of the chaotic hanger bay. Tuskerons ran back and forth directing numerus dropships and barges to land. After the hanger bay was full, the warship turned and jumped into subspace.

"Report," Cameron said to Sargus.

"We're on route back to Camus. Ferrell and Sheridan are still on the Tuskeron Flagship and will meet us back at the compound," Sargus replied.

"If you need me, I'll be in my quarters," Cameron responded.

Without another word, she left the hanger bay and made her way to the guest quarters on the ship. As she approached, her pace increased with every step. She ran to the door. She quickly opened it and slammed it shut behind her. The guest quarters were small and cramped, only enough room for a single Tuskeron.

Cameron made her way to the bathroom and took off her hood. She glanced at the mirror and was shocked and mortified by the sight before her. Blood smeared over her face. Not only her opponent's, but her own as well. Her face was swollen, and her jaw ached.

Cameron slowly took off her battle worn clothes and dropped her white blood-stained shirt on the floor. She continued to her mud-covered boots and cargo pants. She glanced at the mirror but had even more resentment for the mess of a Ranger in front of her. Cameron grit her teeth in anger at the sight of her nano-brand. A circle with three planets and a capital F.

Cameron shook her head and walked into the high ceiling shower. She turned the water on which poured like heavy rain from above. The cold burst took her breath away but in a few seconds the water warmed, and steam crept along the roof. As the temperature rose it filled the entire room and made it difficult to see. Cameron turned the water up higher to the point of burning.

The tranquil water soaked into Cameron's brown hair and flowed over her tanned skin. She looked down at her bare feet and saw the red and brown colored water beneath them. It brought back the memory of the Ranger-Speedster only an hour before. Her body lying there, blood pouring out of the gash in her head. Cameron shut her eyes and turned her sight to the grey tile wall desperately trying to rid herself of the memory, but the image stayed clear and refused to leave.

This was not the first time Cameron had killed one of her own race, but it was the first time she had killed in close quarters in one on one combat. Cameron raised her hands to eye level. Through the downpour she saw her palms shake uncontrollably. She tightened her fists and tried to calm her nerves, but it was no use.

"No matter what you say, destructions on its way. That's what you get when you treat them like a slave," Cameron sang softly, "now stand up, and make the bastards pay. Say it with me now, yes, destructions on its way."

The musical number had been written by Dangerous Doug before the fall of Rydon. Cameron had always liked the artist. Not for his average beat, but because of the lyrics behind it. Destructions on its Way spoke against the Slave Lords and nearly called Ferrell by name.

The Telekinetic's thoughts were interrupted by the sound of her comm ringing. She turned off the water and wrapped a large towel around herself. With her hair dripping on the floor Cameron walked barefoot to her pants and pulled out her comm.

"This is Cameron," she said in a hastened tone, and secured the towel around her thin frame.

"I heard what happened, glad to hear you're alright Cammy," Alex's voice sounded.

"Yeah, it was a hard fight, but I'm doing better," she replied and hid her true feelings.

"I hear congratulations are in order," Alex said to the female Ranger's surprise.

"Congratulations for what?" Cameron inquired.

"I thought you heard, the opening numbers are in and your team had one of the highest capture rates per capita planet wide. Ferrell wanted to pass on his admiration as well," Alex replied.

"Thank you," Cameron responded and did not know how she felt about the news.

"He also wanted to know if you would join us and the other Slave Lords for a celebration dinner?"

Cameron thought about the offer for a moment. It sounded fun and at least she would get out of her room.

"Will I be going as Ferrell's bodyguard or as myself?" Cameron questioned.

"Just as yourself, Cameron. If you want to leave you can at any point, but I would not mind having a few drinks with you," Alex replied.

"Sounds like fun," Cameron said in more of a cheerful tone.

"Well get some rest little one, and I'll see you back at the compound."

The line went dead, and Cameron put the comm on the sink.

A party, Cameron thought to herself.

She was still surprised by the invite. In the three years she had been on Camus, this was the first time she had gone as a guest to a social gathering. Cameron continued to dry herself and made her way out into the room. She put on a clean pair of shorts and a tank top. Cameron pulled a container of AHC out of her bag and walked barefoot to the bed. She sat down and spread the mixture over her face and hands.

"Hopefully, I won't look like shit for the party," Cameron said to herself.

Cameron's thoughts continued to drift.

"Maybe I'll meet some nice man who will free me from slavery and pronounce himself to be mine forever."

Cameron knew it was a fantasy at the best and a delusion at worst.

"At least I'll get to have a few drinks with Alex."

The thought brought a smile to the young Ranger's face. In the years she had been on Camus, Cameron had grown to care and deeply respect the Energy-Caster.

Doesn't help he's handsome, Cameron thought and admitted her crush.

She put down the container of healing cream and laid on the bed. Her eyes closed and she drifted off to sleep praying the day would improve.

* * *

Night had fallen over the compound. It had been three hours since Ferrell and the rest of the fleet had returned to Camus. During that time Cameron had watched what seemed like an endless amount of slave barges. One by one the ships landed and unloaded their hold.

Overall, it made her sick. Thousands of Humans led like sheep, condemned to a life of slavery. Her actions added to the nausea she felt.

Cameron turned and left her room. She walked through the hallways of the compound and made her way to the second great hall.

The Telekinetic had changed soon after returning and was wearing blue jeans, combat boots, white cap shirt and her brown leather blazer. Her hair was out of its normal ponytail and hung at full length. It sat along her cheek bones and had a slight curl.

Cameron had put on extra make up and tried to cover up the bruising on her face. After walking for a few minutes, she came to a set of double doors with two Tuskeron's standing guard. The guards nodded at Cameron and opened the doors. She walked through the frame and found herself in the great hall. It was beautiful. Tile floor with fountains, statues and other forms of artwork placed strategically around the room.

She walked down the small set of stairs and observed the room before her. The Slave Lords stayed spread out, each one in their own conversation. Aden and Conrad were in the center drinking and laughing while Ferrell and Alexandria stood off to the side quietly talking. Colin and his fearsome Accaren bodyguard Damarious stood over by the entrance to the kitchen. A chill went up her spine as their eyes met.

Cameron quickly looked away from Colin, but his gaze stayed fixed on her. This made Cameron even more uncomfortable. For years men had ogled at her attractive build, long legs and flawless face. In her mind this felt different. She was not sure why, but it was. The Ranger did what she could to brush off the feelings and made her way over to Alex. He sat comfortably at the bar on the far side of the great hall.

"Hey Cammy, take a seat," Alex said and greeted her with a warm smile.

"What can I get you?" the female bartender asked in a polite tone.

Cameron looked over the selections for a moment, but her choice was clear.

"Heritage rum please," Cameron said with a smile, requesting one of her people's favorite drinks.

"How would you like that, hun?" the bartender replied and leaned on the counter.

"Neat," Cameron said to Alex's joy.

"Good girl. At least you learned one good thing from me," he commented with a grin.

"What, how to drink?" Cameron replied with a crooked smile.

"How to drink liquor the right way," Alex replied and corrected her.

"Very true," Cameron agreed.

Alex lifted his glass in celebration.

"To the raid of Araka. We went in, kicked ass and somehow made it out of there," he said in a dry sarcastic tone.

"As the Human's say, cheers." Cameron replied and tapped the edge of her glass against his.

She took a sip of her drink and gave out a mild cough.

"Burn?" Alex chuckled.

"Oh, it's good," Cameron giggled and took another drink with a laugh.

"Always been one of my favorites," Alex said and took a sip as well.

Cameron finished her drink and gave a slight shake of her head as she swallowed the bittersweet rum. She set her glass back down and turned her eyes to the mirrored shelf of liquor behind the bar counter. She noticed Alex look down at his glass and could tell he was slightly embarrassed she had finished her drink before him.

"Bottoms up," he proclaimed and downed the whisky.

He set down his glass and motioned for the bartender to return.

"Having the same Cammy, or are you changing it up?" he asked.

"Human rye whisky, straight shot," Cameron replied after a moment.

"Same," Alex said to the bartender, "and please make those doubles."

"Coming right up," the Human woman replied.

She pulled out two shot glasses from behind the counter and an old faded bottle. The bartender poured a double for each and placed them in front of the Rangers.

Alex pulled a handful of Accaren Ingots from his pocket and tipped her well.

"Thank you," he said with a wink and a boyish smile.

"Anytime Alex," the bartender replied in a playful manner.

Cameron could not help but notice the woman's flirtatious smile and observed her hand brush over her mentor's face as she made her way back to the bar.

"Have you ever been married, Alex?" Cameron asked out of the blue.

"No, but I loved a Ranger once who I'm sure has forgotten all about me."

"What was she like?" Cameron pressed eagerly and picked up her drink.

"Fierce, beautiful and loyal, but blind to the reality of life," Alex replied.

He picked up his drink and prepared to toast.

"Don't worry Cammy, when your ready we'll find you some nice boy or girl to play around with. Believe me you're better off single," Alex said and took his shot.

Cameron had no idea what to think or say and quickly downed her drink. She could feel herself blush and hoped Alex would think it was just the alcohol.

"Another," Alex called to the bartender and payed his gratuity in advance.

Cameron looked down at the ever-increasing amount of Accaren currency he gave. She pondered for a moment and looked up at him with a confused expression.

"I promise it will be worth it," Alex whispered down to her, "drinking rule number seven Cammy, always tip your bar tender well. It will benefit you in a multiplicity of ways."

"Cameron," Ferrell's voice sounded from behind them.

She and Alex turned to see the Slave Lord approach from the center of the room. He appeared inebriated and drifted from side to side as he walked.

"Good work today," he proclaimed and gave her a kind pat on the back.

"Thank you," Cameron replied not sure what to think of his happiness.

"Have either of you seen Nora?" Ferrell asked and referred to his personal slave.

Cameron and Alex both shook their heads in response.

"Cameron could you find Nora, and have her start the main course?" Ferrell commanded.

He glanced around in a paranoid fashion and leaned closer to the Rangers.

"I just want to feed these assholes and get them off my world," he whispered, "you would never belief how much I miss Reid Masters right now."

"I'm sure," Alex chuckled.

"Ferrell," Conrad's whiney voice sounded from across the room, "I have another wager for you."

Ferrell took a deep frustrated breath and clenched his jaw.

"Find her," he said in a firmer tone and walked back to the young Slave Lord.

Cameron downed the rest of her shot and hopped off the barstool.

"Order another, I'll be right back," she said with an infectious smile.

"Don't' worry I'll be waiting for you," Alex returned in kind and motioned for the bar tender to join him for a shot.

Cameron turned and made her way over to the kitchen. Upon entering she saw tables lining the room. The food sat nicely prepared on china plates, but Nora was nowhere to be seen.

"Nora," Cameron called out.

No response. In the back Cameron saw lights on in one of the storerooms and quickly made her way forward down the dimly lit hallway.

"Nora? Are you there?" Cameron asked as she walked through the door to the pantry.

Cameron let out a gasp at the sight before her. Nora was lying on the floor. Her clothes ripped asunder, and she had been savagely beaten.

"Cameron," the woman murmured in pain.

Gods, she's been raped. Cameron panicked in her mind. She rushed forward and tried to help but Nora pulled her knees to her chest and backed up tight against the wall.

"Nora, who did this to you?" Cameron asked in a soft tone.

"Slave Lord," the woman whispered.

Panic filled Nora's face as her eyes darted to the door. Cameron whipped around and saw the enormous figure of Colin Trails. There was a sickening smile on his face as his sinister black eyes lusted over her.

"We are property of James Ferrell, Slave Lord and ruler of Camus. You will let us pass," Cameron postured.

"Well aren't you just full of fire. You're going to be fun to break in," he sneered.

Cameron and Nora became trapped as Colin continued to block the path. Cameron knew she could not use her Ranger abilities due to the amount of witnesses, one of which being a Slave Lord. Cameron reached for her comm, but Colin lunged forward and slapped the device out of her hand. Cameron balled up her fist and cracked Colin across the jaw.

The Slave Lord's head whipped to the side. He turned back with even more hatred fueled by her assault.

He countered in similar fashion and struck the left of Cameron's face. The sheer strength of the hit threw Cameron to the floor.

The teen Ranger struggled to her feet but was immediately backhanded on her right side. She lost her balance and crashed into the wall. Blood ran out of her nose and mouth. Her vision was blurred as her head continued to spin.

Cameron felt Colin's rough hand around her throat. She gasped for air, but he merely gripped tighter. She fought back and punched him in the gut and ribs. But Colin pushed her to the back wall and pulled off her leather jacket. Another strike to the face brought the Ranger down to the cold floor.

She wanted desperately to use her ascension. She could win, easily.

Grind him into the floor, she thought with hatred.

"Alex," Cameron gasped as Colin slapped her again.

Colin held her down. He climbed on top, ripped Cameron's white shirt and exposed her bra.

"I'm going to enjoy every inch of you," Colin hissed.

Cameron screamed out in terror, but the strong man put his hand over her mouth and silenced her. This was Cameron's worst nightmare, and everything had spiraled out of control.

"Keep fighting," Colin snapped as he unbuttoned her pants.

Cameron saw a figure in a white shirt. A second later, the figure ripped her attacker off and slammed him against the side wall.

The battered Ranger desperately tried to cover herself and turned to the doorway.

Alex Sheridan held a magnificent pose. He had Colin pinned against the door with his forearm pressed tightly against the Human's throat.

Cameron had never seen Alex in an all-out rage, but she thanked the gods he had come.

"Stupid Human bastard!" Alex screamed at the top of his lungs, "I'm going to break every bone in your body and feed your remains to our Draith slaves!"

Colin lit up with a fury of his own. He lifted Alex off the ground and slammed the Ranger into the adjacent doorframe.

Alex regained his footing and countered with a three-hit combo. Two of the attacks hit Colin in the ribs while the third impacted directly above his right knee.

Colin lost his balance and fell toward the hallway. On the way down Alex fired an Energy punch and struck the Human directly in the chest. The hit lifted Colin off the ground and threw him back into the kitchen.

Alex paused for the briefest of moments but could not bring himself to look at Cameron. Rage once again filled his face as he took off in a dead sprint for Colin.

Cameron quickly backed up to the corner and franticly tried to secure her torn shirt. She struggled to her feet and pulled her blouse around her. She made her way to the door and peeked into the kitchen. Both Ranger and Human crashed around the room and back into the great hall.

Cameron ran forward to the main door but stopped dead in her tracks as an orange Accaren shield blast fired across her path. To her left, Alex stood back up after the hit by the stunning weapon. His eyes fixed on Damarious, Colin's Accaren bodyguard. The rest of the Slave Lords staggered around the room and watched the event unfold. Blue energy swirled around Alex's fists and was prepared to fight the armored guard to reach his true target.

"What's going on?" Ferrell's voice boomed.

The lead Slave Lord stopped dead in his tracks as his eyes met with Cameron's. He looked over her bruised and bloodied face and saw she was holding back tears as well as her shirt. In that moment, his expressions turned from anger to rage. He glanced at Alex who was still in a standoff with the Accaren.

"You sick, perverted, dog shit eating douche bag," Ferrell yelled over to the opposing Slave Lord, "I always knew you were a depraved inbred son of a bitch, but this?"

Colin was infuriated by Ferrell's insult and the snide question that followed. He stepped forward in front of his bodyguard.

"What did you say, James," Colin hissed and stepped even closer.

Ferrell boldly matched the man's pace and stood toe to toe in the center of the hall.

"Did you really think you could come in here and take what you want?" Ferrell yelled up at the Human giant, "use my slaves, disrespect me in my own fortress?"

"Maybe it's time for a change in leadership," Colin proclaimed, "and the old should be put to rest."

Ferrell paused at the statement.

"The one thing you're not going to do Colin, is threaten me on my own damn planet," Ferrell retorted in a sharp tone.

"I just did," Colin fired back.

"I am James Ferrell, ranking Slave Lord, ruler of Camus and member of the Ninth Faction Council. You will pay for any damages done and will apologize for the abuse on my slaves," Ferrell yelled back.

"And if I don't?" Colin growled.

"Then you will be lucky to leave this hall alive and will be at war with the Ninth Faction," Ferrell threatened.

"War it is," Colin snapped, "anyone else ready for a change? If so, follow me!"

Colin turned and walked toward the door, closely followed by his bodyguard. Soon after Alexandria followed the rogue Slave Lord to Ferrell's disgust. The Tuskerons escorted them out of the hall and in the direction of the landing pad.

"Well this is going to complicate things," Conrad whined.

"Shut up, Conrad," Ferrell snapped.

The Slave Lord turned to his enforcer and head of security.

"I need to make a call. Escort Aden and Conrad to the tactical center. I will be there shortly," Ferrell commanded and walked briskly out of the great hall.

Alex and Cameron's eyes met. She could see the pain and anger in his expressions. Cameron turned her head and walked briskly out of the hall. As soon as she left Alex's sight, her walk turned into a jog and finally into an all-out sprint. Cameron threw open the door of her room and slammed it behind her. The lock latched, and Cameron broke down into tears. The assaulted Ranger pressed the back of her head against the door and sat down on the tile floor. Cameron put her hands over her face.

"Gods!" she screamed and tried to abolish the feeling of his hands on her, "I could have stopped him. I could have crushed him with a stroke of my hand!"

Cameron used her ability to hurl a small table next to her. The furniture flew forward at remarkable speed and crashed out on the balcony. Upon impact it broke into a dozen pieces.

"Cameron?" Alex's voice sounded through the door.

"Go away," she yelled defensively.

Cameron slammed her head against the door in anger and frustration, but there was only silence on the other end.

"I really don't want to talk right now, Alex," Cameron replied and tried to hide her emotional state.

"I just…" Alex trailed off, "I just wanted to make sure you're alright."

"I'm fine," Cameron quickly replied and tried not to burst into tears at the thought.

"If you need something, you know where to find me," Alex said in a calming tone.

Cameron did not answer and sat in silence hands still covering her bloodied face.

"For the record Cameron, it pains me to say this, but you made the right choice by not using your abilities," Alex said empathetically, "I am so very proud of your strength and your courage."

Cameron heard him walk away and left her alone once again. She rested her head against the door. It had already been a rough day, but deep down she knew it was only the beginning.

Now the Slave Lords were at war.

LEVEL 5

Cameron ran at top speed through a dark, stone-built tunnel. The walls and roof looked the same with no exit to be found. Cameron could barely see two meters in front of her but kept running.

She stopped at an intersection in the path. There were three different hallways to choose from. The Telekinetic peered out but each one appeared the same. Cameron's heart pounded as she stood and gasped for air.

Her adrenaline spiked at the sound of heavy footsteps behind her. Cameron frantically looked down each path trying to find a way out but was still unsure. The footsteps became louder and forced the teen Ranger to decide.

Cameron turned and sprinted down the right tunnel in hopes of escaping the maze and the stranger behind her. Every time the Ranger had tried to evade her stalker, the sound of their terrifying footsteps echoed off the walls of the stone tunnel.

The female Ranger stopped dead in her tracks at the sight before her. It was a dead end. Cameron rushed up and searched for a hidden door but there was none. Her breathing had increased and was at the point of hyperventilating. Cameron whipped around. She was prepared to double back but froze as her eyes fell upon a shadowed figure standing a half-dozen-meters from her.

The man was tall and had a husky build. His face was shrouded by the low light levels and concealed his identity.

"Stay away from me!" Cameron yelled defensively.

The stranger ignored her warning and aggressively moved forward.

"Get back!" Cameron screamed at the top of her lungs.

She raised her hands and attempted to access her ascension, but the man continued forward unfazed.

He finally came into sight. Cameron gasped as she saw the face of Colin Trails.

"I'm going to enjoy every inch of you," Colin sneered in a malicious tone.

Cameron balled her fists as Colin moved toward her. She leapt forward and struck him across the jaw. She made a quick recovery and landed an outer leg kick. It was well placed and threw her opponent off balance. The thinly built Ranger used the opening and leapt to Colin's left. If Cameron could get past him here, she would have a chance to make it back to the intersection.

She felt a tug on her right arm and Cameron whipped around. Colin's fist slammed into her jaw. Cameron's head snapped to the side. Colin gripped her buy the hair and arm to the point of pain, but Cameron was not through. She balled up her right fist and swung with all her might. The right hook slammed into Colin's jaw, but did little damage.

Clearly angered by her resistance, Colin pulled her around and threw her against the dead-end wall. Cameron slumped to the ground with blood pouring out of her nose and down her face.

Cameron pushed off against the wall and preformed a roundhouse kick. Her leg swung with purpose and struck Colin in the ribs. He was not harmed by her perfect assault and stood fast. He gripped ahold of her leg, lifted the hundred- and ten-pound Ranger into the air and slammed her into the stone floor. Cameron's head hit the ground and she was out cold.

* * *

Cameron awoke from the dream and sat up in her bed as objects floated around. The Telekinetic's ability would manifest in her sleep and lifted small to medium objects around her. A few crashes sounded as Cameron's comm and other items fell to the tile floor.

Her hands were raised in defense, eyes darting around her room. Cameron's face, boy shorts, tank top and hair were drenched in sweat at the nightmare her eyes had seen.

"Gods," she gasped and put her hands over her face, "it was so real."

It had been two months since the raid on Araka and the horror that followed. In that time the dynamic between the Slave Lords had changed. Colin Trails and Alexandria Morgan had rebelled against Ferrell's leadership which ignited the war of the Slave Lords.

Soon after the fight on Camus, Colin and Alexandria secured their territories in the old Accaren Empire. They were first to draw blood and attacked the Ninth Factions holdings on TS-2, Syprus, and raided over two dozen slave convoys in the first week. In the month that followed, both sides took heavy losses in the shipping lanes. Not to mention dozens of warships and hundreds of troops.

Cameron stood up and made her way into the bathroom. She rested her hands on the sink and looked at the mirror. Her face was red, and her hair was a mess. She took a handful of cold water and splashed it over her face. After not getting the results she had hoped for, Cameron repeated the process.

After her head cleared, Cameron returned to her bedroom.

"What time is it anyway?" she asked and made her way to a clock.

"Oh good, it's two in the morning," she muttered.

Cameron sat on the edge of the bed and felt frustrated. She had been having nightmares since the event at the party. Each one was the same, she was trapped and could not use her ascension.

"It's what it is," Cameron said in a depressed tone.

The compound shook with fury as a large explosion sounded. Cameron reached down and picked her comm off the floor.

"Cameron to Alex. What's going on?" she said into the device.

"We have a situation. Get your tactical gear and meet me in the lion's den ASAP," Alex commanded.

"Understood," Cameron replied.

She turned off the comm and tossed it on the bed. Cameron stood up and rushed over to her wardrobe. She pulled out her jeans, purple tank top, energy-pistol and combat boots. She quickly dressed and grabbed her leather coat on the way out. Cameron sprinted down the hallway of the compound and secured her hood as she went. It did not take her long to reach the powerlift. The doors shut, and Cameron started a rapid descent to the lower levels.

After she reached her destination, the Telekinetic walked out onto a metal bridge which overlooked the lion's den.

Cameron looked down at the slave pit and saw both Human and Accaren prisoners locked in their cells. To her left Cameron saw Alex address four squads of Tuskeron's. They stood in a circle around the Energy-Caster and remained silent. Cameron walked to her left, down the metal stairs and over to the group. The Tuskeron stepped to the side and allowed her to pass.

"Morning Cammy," Alex addressed her in a direct tone, "ten minutes ago, we recorded a massive explosion on level five."

Level five. Built to house the most dangerous of Ferrell's slaves.

"At this point, levels one through four are locked down. Our mission is to secure the block. Dead or alive. Alright get to it!" Alex proclaimed.

The Tuskerons split up into squads and walked over to the gun racks on the wall.

This left Alex, Sargus and Cameron in a triangle.

"What happened?" Cameron asked and took a step closer to Alex.

"Don't know. We lost contact with the entire level," he replied in a concerned tone.

"What's down there?" Cameron asked, intrigued by the information.

Alex looked over at Sargus and then back to her. Cameron could tell by his reactions he tried to find the correct phrasing.

"Do you remember your first day here?" Alex asked and crossed his arms.

Cameron looked to the side and tried to recall the memories. She remembered perfectly. After almost killing Ferrell, the Telekinetic had been locked up on level four.

"I remember hearing voices in my head," Cameron recalled, "you said they were Xan. Have they escaped?"

"Got it in one, kid," he said with a chuckle.

"So, who are the Xan?" Cameron questioned.

"The best way to describe them is comparing them to a Ranger. They have specific abilities ranging from levels one to five, with two major differences. The first is how the classes are setup. For example, a Ranger Fire-Caster compared to a Xan Pyro-Mage. The fifth ascension for a Fire-Caster is inferno. The caster creates a fifteen-yard radius of fire and heat comparable to a Serpent," Alex explained, "the Pyro-Mage on the other hand can raise the temperature of multiple targets, igniting them and anything around them."

"What's the second difference?" Cameron asked tentatively.

"All Xan are telepathic," he replied and motioned for them to move in the direction of the cargo lift, while Sargus rejoined the rest of the hybrids.

"Sargus, take your squad down the main powerlift. Cameron and I will take the back way," Alex commanded.

"Roger," the lead Tuskeron grunted.

He moved forward and motioned for the rest of the rhinos to follow him into the lift. Cameron and Alex entered the slower cargo-lift. They shut the door and started their descent. Cameron took off her hood and started brushing her knotted hair.

"So, what type of Xan will we be facing?" Cameron asked.

"According to the log, there should be one Pyro-Mage and a Mind-Ripper," Alex replied and pulled out a small data-pad.

"A what?" Cameron stammered with wide eyes.

"A Mind-Ripper is the Xan's twisted version of an Empath-Ranger. They can invoke rage, fear, and influence thoughts. Some have even said a Mind-Ripper can transfer a being's consciousness from one body to another," he continued to Cameron's amazement and terror.

The cargo-lift came to a stop, but the doors stayed shut. Alex pulled a holo-map out of his pocket. The fifth level like all the others looped around and formed a horseshoe between the lifts. Directly halfway was a small passageway and room.

"What's in there?" Cameron quietly asked and pointed at the hidden area.

"No idea," Alex replied in a similar tone, "the Xan should be here."

Alex pointed at an area twenty-five yards from the main powerlift and Sargus's team.

"So, we're flanking the Xan?" Cameron confirmed.

"Beautiful, Cammy," Alex said with a smile, "do you sense anything?"

"Yes," she replied with a puzzled look, "they do feel almost like Rangers."

"Be careful, the Xan are from the Orion-Cluster. They are unpredictable and incredibly dangerous," he warned.

Alex motioned for the Telekinetic to prepare herself and pulled up her hood. Cameron raised her hands in defense as Alex opened the door. The hallway was black with minimal lighting, every fifteen meters or so there was another cell carved into the stone wall. Each one was empty and were like the cells she had endured on level four. They moved forward and slowly cleared each compartment as they went. It was silent while Cameron's heart pounded. She felt cold, and shaky.

Where are they? Cameron asked herself.

We're here, a voice replied clear as day.

Caught off guard Cameron stopped dead in her tracks and turned with concern to Alex.

"What's wrong?" he asked.

Free us, the voice said in her mind.

"Alex," Cameron stuttered and tried to talk over the voices, "they're in my head."

Free us! the voice repeated with more intensity.

This time the voices were not just in Cameron's mind but Alex as well.

Roaring from the nearby Tuskerons echoed through the hallway's followed by weapons fire.

"We've taken heavy losses...falling back..." Sargus's deep voice crackled over the comm.

"Sargus do you read?" Alex replied, but there was only static on the other end, "Sargus."

Alex waited but there was still no response.

Free us, the voice said again, angered by their lack of compliance.

*Free us now! t*he voice repeated over and over and continually increased in volume.

Cameron put her hands over her ears, but it was no use. She turned to Alex who suffered the same effect. The volume grew and dropped both Rangers to their knees. Cameron screamed out in pain at the overwhelming sound. It was unbearable.

The voices suddenly stopped and left Cameron and Alex on the ground out of breath. Cameron struggled to her feet and turned back to her mentor who was still on the ground.

"I hate them," he said to himself.

His jaw clenched while his fists tightened, knuckles white from the pressure.

"I hate them all!" he screamed.

"Alex—"

"Shut up!" he yelled and interrupted her.

Cameron was taken aback by his sharp tone and scornful eyes. To the best of her memory she had never seen the Energy-Caster this upset. She looked into his light blue eyes and saw unmeasurable wrath.

"The Mind-Ripper is invoking your rage," Cameron said and quickly figured out the strategy.

"I can't keep them out," he stuttered.

Alex screamed at the top of his lungs and activated his second ascension. A massive shockwave erupted from him. It lifted Cameron off the ground and threw her into the tunnel wall. The female Ranger rolled to the earth. Cameron stumbled to her feet and removed her hood.

"Alex, calm yourself," she said firmly.

"You can't command me, you're a slave," he yelled almost spitting at her.

Cameron felt a deep pit in her stomach as Alex's words cut through her. In that moment she felt terror and true fear. As it grew in her mind all Cameron wanted to do was hide. Alex stood up fists and jaw still clenched. He took a step forward, but Cameron backed away.

"Stay back!" she screamed.

"Or what?" he retorted.

"I don't want to fight you—"

Before Cameron could finish her sentence, Alex threw an energy-burst. It hit her in the shoulder and knocked Cameron to the ground. Alex charged forward, but Cameron took hold of the Ranger, held him midair and threw him in to the wall.

Cameron scrambled to her feet and looked down at Alex who was still recovering. She wanted to stand and fight but was consumed with unimaginable terror. The young Ranger decided to flee and took off in a dead sprint deeper into the level. A sharp pain filled her back and shoulder as Alex caught her with another energy-punch. Cameron stumbled forward but was able to maintain her footing and kept pace. She glanced back and saw Alex running after her.

Cameron skidded to a stop after reaching the rounded halfway point. To her left was a smaller tunnel bored into the wall. Dead ahead was the path to Sargus and the second lift. Cameron slowly made her way forward.

Up to this point she had only sensed the Xan but had not found where they were lurking. She peaked around the corner and saw two Six legged aliens. They were jet black with armored skin. Their heads stretched above their bodies and were almost triangular. Their legs which looked almost like swords dug into the sand.

Oh gods. Cameron thought to herself.

As if she had screamed at the top of her lungs both Xan whipped around and gazed into her fear filled expressions. They had six eyes with a small mouth. Cameron instantly felt their presence in her mind. The Pyro-Mage launched a fireball which barely missed Cameron. She whipped around and hoped to double back, but Alex had reached her.

Seeing no other option Cameron turned and sprinted toward the smaller tunnel.

"Hammer!" she heard Alex yell from behind.

Cameron whipped around to see the Energy-Caster power his fifth ascension. She swept her hand to the side and threw him off balance. The Energy-Hammer flew forward. Cameron used the last of her strength and dove into the tunnel. The Hammer flew into the roof and broke the stone apart. Cameron rolled into the tunnel barely missing the cave in. Dust flew up and blinded the young Ranger for a few seconds. Cameron gazed back at the entrance only to see she was trapped.

"Damn," she said quietly.

The overwhelming fear seemed to dissipate as Cameron inspected her surroundings. Beyond the door the narrow path continued left and seemed to wind deeper into the tunnel. Cameron followed the path and after a few dozen meters found herself in a medium sized room. There was a table and a medical station off to the left, Cameron looked to the right and saw a shielded cell. The barrier appeared to be dimensional shielding. Something the Ranger had only seen once before in her own cell on level four.

The room was far larger than any other holding cell she had seen. As Cameron approached, she noticed it was beautifully decorated and was suited for Human living. She walked forward and stood a meter away from the barrier. Upon closer inspection, she saw two smaller rooms branched off from the main living area. The living room was decorated with a variety of Old Earth technology. There was a small box serving as a monitor with cords coming off the device. The cables stretched about a meter and connected into a primitive gaming system.

The door to the bathroom opened and a petite woman walked out. She had a short athletic build and wore a t-shirt and grey sweatpants. She appeared to be in her early-thirties and did not notice Cameron as she walked back into the living room. The dirty blond made her way forward and plopped down on the couch. She picked up the controller and started playing the combat simulator. After a few seconds she paused the game and turned to Cameron

"Who the hell are you?" she asked in a blunt tone.

"I'm not the one who's locked in a cage," Cameron retorted.

The woman glared over at her response. She stood up, walked over to the shield and stood directly across from the shrouded Ranger.

"Well I wouldn't be stuck in this quaint little hell hole if an immortal dickhead hadn't imprisoned me here," the woman ranted, "do you want to know the sick part? That twisted cousin screwing douche-waffle decorated this cows shit pile like my old apartment back on Earth."

Cameron chuckled at the woman's creative cursing and tilted her head to the side with confusion by the ending statement.

"You mean New Earth?" Cameron clarified.

"No sweet pea, I mean the original, the blue marble, the place of mankind's origin," she retorted in a condescending tone.

"But the Humans evacuated Old Earth two hundred years ago," Cameron questioned.

The Telekinetic used her second ability and sensed the aura of the strange woman. Although the shield made it difficult Cameron could feel she was Human.

"As a friend of mine likes to say, I'm older than I look," she replied with warmer inflections, "Shelby Pierce, I'd shake your hand but like I said, he's a dick."

"Cameron Summers. So, who locked you down here and why?" the Ranger pressed.

"The who is easy. Adrian Quin. The why on the other hand is a much longer story. Putting it simply he was a bit obsessed with me, and not in a healthy way."

Cameron took off her hood. She brushed her stray hairs back into her ponytail and checked herself for injuries.

Shelby examined Cameron from head to toe.

"Yep you're a cutie. What are you doing in a God forsaken place like this?" Shelby asked.

"Adrian Quin, short, blond hair, arrogant—" Cameron started.

"He's also a cold, calculating psychopath," Shelby cut in and finished her sentence, "how the hell do you know Adrian?"

Shelby crossed her arms and was surprised by Cameron's knowledge.

"I travel," Cameron replied cryptically.

"Adrian's a paranoid, reclusive pot head with a mild obsession to coke, and that was before we created the Crimson Syndicate. How did you survive meeting one of the most dangerous men in all of Known-Space and the Orion-Cluster?" Shelby pressed.

"I'm very careful when I travel," Cameron rephrased and held her ground.

Confusion filled Shelby's face as she tried to figure out the riddle.

"I sensed Adrian is Human. I can also tell your Human as well. How do you have abilities and what is the Crimson Syndicate?" Cameron redirected.

Shelby was once again floored by Cameron's statement and started pacing back and forth. Her eyes fixed on the floor.

"I don't get it, who the hell are you?" Shelby asked with confusion.

"My name is Cameron Lynn Summers. First ascension Telekinetic and Sense-Ranger," she replied and gave her formal title.

"Oh," Shelby replied with a blank stare, "I bet you two had an interesting conversation."

"It was," Cameron replied.

"And now I'm getting you want me to answer your question?" the blond woman asked.

Cameron merely gave a nod of her head.

"Fine," Shelby whined.

She walked over to the fridge and pulled out a can which appeared to be a beverage. It opened with a hiss and Shelby took a few chugs. She let out a deep breath and made her way back to the shield.

"What is it?" Cameron inquired.

"It's called beer, and it's always been a good friend," Shelby answered and took another drink, "now I'm ready for story time. What do you want to know?"

Cameron took a second to consider her options, but in the end, there was only one choice. It was the same question she had asked herself the first time Alex had told her about Adrian.

"What's the Crimson Syndicate?" Cameron inquired.

"There are six of us total. Adrian Quin, Alyssa Brittain, Candice Loc, Wesley Travis, and Trevor Michaelson. We were born on Earth over a thousand years ago. It was a time and place absent modern technology and at that point Humans thought they were the center of the universe."

Cameron smiled at the comment. She stayed silent and allowed Shelby to continue.

"Well somewhere along the line, Adrian, Alyssa and Trevor became obsessed with demonology and through that started down a dark path. I don't want to call them spells because there is more science behind it," Shelby explained.

She finished her beer, crushed the can and tossed it perfectly into a trash can a few meters away.

"Score!" Shelby exclaimed.

She walked back to the fridge and pulled out another beer.

"After the Accaren war and the Humans coming into Known-Space, Adrian made a discovery. He found the Valari."

Cameron stood in shock and awe at the answer. She had heard about the vampiric aliens in school. They were dimensional beings who could possess aliens on this side of the vale.

"So, your saying Adrian summoned Valari to Known-Space?" Cameron clarified.

"He opened the door," Shelby confirmed.

She took another large drink.

` "Finally buzzed," the dirty blond said with a smile, "but anyway, back to the story. There is a thirty percent difference between the energy Adrian pulls compared to say myself. After opening himself up to the Valari dimension, Adrian changed. He created the Ninth Faction and has done what he can to bring back slavery and take over Known-Space."

She finished the second beer and tossed it in the trash with the same perfect accuracy.

"But do you want to know the really screwed up part? It's his worship to that demon bitch Elyzabeth."

Pain filled Cameron's mind and she put her hands over her ears. The Xan had returned. Cameron could feel their presence at a far greater intensity.

"They broke through the rocks," Cameron said to herself.

"Who broke through the rocks?" Shelby questioned.

Still in pain, Cameron glanced up with disgust and surprise.

"With everything you just told me, with all your abilities you don't know the Xan are coming?" Cameron spouted back.

"I'm Human and even with my abilities at full strength I can only sense dimensional energy." Shelby replied, "If you're a Telekinetic you may just be able to get me out of here."

"Why would I do that?" Cameron questioned.

"Because you'll never be able to defeat them by yourself," Shelby argued.

Cameron looked deeply into the woman's eyes and tried to gauge her intent. Cameron saw a longing to be free, something she related to deeply. She took a step back and observed the shield. The barrier appeared to be built into the door frame and did not have a visible way of deactivating it. Cameron lifted her hands and attempted to disrupt the shield. Nothing happened. Cameron tried her ascension again, but the walls merely shook.

Cameron yelled out in frustration.

"There should be a power junction a half meter to your left," Shelby said and pointed at the wall.

Cameron's eyesight ran along the wall and finally saw the junction, but the technology was foreign to her.

"I found it!" Cameron exclaimed.

"Perfect," Shelby yelled through the shield, "now you should see a small cover you can pull off."

Cameron looked over the wall and saw the cover. She tried to remove it, but it would not budge.

"It's sealed shut," Cameron yelled back.

"I hate that son of a bitch so much," Shelby cursed in frustration.

"Is there another way I can—"

Cameron was cut off by a fireball which whipped past her head. She turned her gaze and saw both Xan standing in the shadows. She used her ability to pick up the Mind-Ripper. She held the six-legged alien for a split second and slammed its body into the Pyro-Mage. Both aliens slumped to the ground and bought Cameron a few seconds.

She whipped around in search of her next plan. Deeper in the cave the Telekinetic saw a dozen large rocks resting on the earth. She took a step back, stretched for her hand and hurled the largest one at the control panel. Sparks flew up on impact and blinded Cameron for a split second. She looked up and saw the shield flicker before it failed completely. Still seeing stars, she saw the silhouette of Shelby walk out of the cell.

Shelby whispered an unknown phrase and her eyes lit up with bright orage. She repeated it over and over. Cameron listened intently and realized it was Latin. An ancient Old Earth dialect that had died off thousands of years before. Ferrell had introduced Old Earth history into Cameron's classes a few years back. These included basics of Latin, but from what Alex had said this was not common, even for Humans.

The ground shook and wisps of orange colored energy formed around her. Shelby's muscles tensed up for a second as the energy absorbed into her body. Cameron covered her ears as the Xan screamed out in frustration, but Shelby was unaffected. She stood in front of Cameron, hands on her hips.

"Your telepathy won't work on me," she sneered.

"Syndicate," the lead Xan hissed.

The voice sent a chill up Cameron's spine and sounded like a whisper.

"Yes, I am, and your tiny minds should know what I am capable of," Shelby replied in a firm tone.

Cameron gazed up at Shelby and then back to the Xan. She could see in their black eyes they were weighing their options. Without warning the right Xan lifted its arm and launched three fireballs simultaneously. The Mind-Ripper charged forward to face Shelby in hand to hand combat.

The fireballs whizzed forward and slammed into Shelby's shield. The flames engulfed her upper body for a split second. As the flames subsided, Cameron could see Shelby's orange dimensional shield absorb the burning inferno. Shelby stood unfazed by the attack and took off for the Mind-Ripper.

The smoke cleared, and Cameron could see the second Xan. The alien used the flames as a distraction and was within a meter of the Human woman. The glassy black alien towered over her by a half meter. The width of its leg span stood equal to Shelby's height. The alien swung with all its might, but Shelby eloquently dodged the assault. Predicting her maneuver, the Xan countered with one of its spider-like arms.

It swung across, but to Cameron's amazement Shelby ducked under the attack and with one fluid motion pulled back her right arm. Dimensional energy swirled around her forearm. She cried out and threw a massive punch. Her shielded-punch collided with the Mind-Ripper. It lifted the alien off the ground and crashed into the roof before it landed dead next to the Pyro-Mage.

A horrified scream echoed through the narrow passageway.

"Marine Corps bitch!" Shelby yelled with fiery expression.

Although Cameron had no idea what she meant, the Ranger adored the passion behind the war cry. Shelby continued her assault and threw an orange ball of energy. The Pyro-Mage was unable to dodge and was hit directly. The Xan slammed against the wall and fell to the ground. Before the alien could recover, Shelby threw two additional spheres. They hit with such force Cameron could hear the alien's bones break.

Cameron sat up still in amazement at the events that had transpired. Shelby walked over to her and extended her hand.

"Need some help?" she asked.

Cameron gave a half smile and gripped her forearm. Shelby helped the Ranger back to her feet. She ran back into the cell, grabbed two beers, and made a quick getaway into the hallway. Shelby opened the first and chugged the entirety of the can. When she was finished, she crushed it and threw it back into the cell.

"God that felt good!" Shelby exclaimed, "it has been way to long since I've hit something. Way to long since I've been free. Thank you Cameron I owe you one."

"That was amazing," Cameron replied still in shock.

Shelby just smiled.

"So how did a sweet girl like you start working for Ferrell?" the Syndicate member asked.

"Well working for is not the best word, I'm a—" Cameron started, but Shelby raised her hand and silenced her.

"That brazen asshole," Shelby said to herself.

"What?" Cameron asked.

"Don't you sense it?" Shelby retorted.

Cameron closed her eyes and focused her mind. She pressed through the lingering pain of the mental attacks and felt the presence of Adrian. He was down the hallway and got closer by the second.

"Gods," Cameron said matching her expressions.

"I'm sorry," Shelby apologized.

Cameron cocked her head unsure of Shelby's meaning. Before Cameron could react, Shelby threw a jab and struck her mouth and nose. The Ranger's head snapped back. Cameron stretched out her arm, but before she could use her ability Shelby interlocked her fingers behind Cameron's neck and thrusted her knee in to the Telekinetic's gut. She repeated the process two more times and made sure the Ranger was incapacitated.

Cameron fell to her knees coughing with her hands on her stomach. She peered up at Shelby with confusion.

"Stay down," she said and landed a right hook across Cameron's jaw.

The Ranger's body slammed against the hard earth. Her lip was cracked with blood pouring out of her mouth and nose. In the distance Cameron could see three blurred figures standing down the hallway. As her eyes focused, she saw Alex and Ferrell with Adrian standing in front of them.

"Hello Shelby," Adrian said.

"Filthy impotent cock sucker!" Shelby screamed.

"You know damn well I'm not impotent."

"Fuck you Adrian!" she screamed in response and flipped him off.

The curse was unfamiliar to Cameron and she had no idea what it meant.

"Wow, haven't heard that word in a while," Adrian said fondly and was not offended, "how did you get free?"

"Your Xan friends shut off the power. I killed them, and then your Ranger bitch tried to stop me," she lied.

"Cameron," Alex said.

"She's okay," Shelby replied, "funny you would keep a Telekinetic with your checkered past."

"I don't fear her just as I don't' fear you," Adrian proclaimed and stepped forward.

"Shut it dick weed!" Shelby fired back.

Her face lit up with anger. She cocked back her arm and fired a dimensional sphere into Adrian's shield. He stumbled back and gave a shake of his head.

"You're just the same obsessive, arrogant, self-absorbed boy you've always been!" she yelled.

A moment of silence followed.

"I'm going to leave, Adrian," Shelby announced, "I'm going to find Trevor, Alyssa and the rest of our friends. I'm going to tell them what you did to me, and then I'm going to come back and kick your skinny, white, German ass!"

As a final act of defiance, Shelby flipped him off. Before Adrian could respond, an orange cyclone surrounded Shelby. Arcs of lightning struck the earth and in the blink of an eye the tornado vanished.

Through her haze, Cameron could see Adrian glare at Ferrell.

"Throne room," Adrian commanded, "now."

Ferrell grit his teeth and followed the Syndicate member back to the main hallway.

Alex rushed forward and knelt at Cameron's side. He put his strong arms around her and helped the wounded Ranger to her feet.

"I'm so sorry, Cammy. They got to me," he said in a mournful tone.

"I know the feeling," Cameron coughed.

"About what I said—"

"It's fine," she interrupted and cut him off.

She put her hand on her head and tried to ignore the massive headache Shelby had given her.

"Let's get you back to your room."

Alex lifted Cameron off the ground. He held her in his powerful arms and carried the half-conscious teen back to the safety of the fortress. Away from the nightmare on level five.

VENGEANCE

Deep on the far side of Ninth Faction space an ominous sight could be seen in the pale light. It was a Tuskeron fleet. The light off the white dwarf star reflected off the vessels grey hull causing them to glimmer. Over thirty ships strong, a true force to be reckoned with. Their engines were off and remained motionless in perfect formation.

Inside the Flagship, Cameron stood around a large holo-map of Daigys Prime.

A few days before, Ferrell had received information that Colin Trails had moved many slaves to the planet and had decided to transfer them to his upcoming buyers off world.

Cameron wore her black leather coat. The hood was pulled tightly over her head and concealed her face from sight with help from the holo emitters along the inner lining.

Alex stood to her right. His arms crossed with his gaze fixed on the map. Ferrell, Conrad and Maglar stood across from the Rangers. For the past hour, the group had debated a plan of attack but had failed thus far to reach a conclusion.

"I agree with Maglar," Conrad whined, "the only way this is even worth it is to attack during the slave transfer. That way we can double our profit."

Ferrell rolled his eyes at the over simplified reiteration.

"Conrad, that was always part of the plan," Ferrell retorted, "once again, we have an opportunity to balance the scales with that bastard Trails. For the past year we have lost millions of Accaren Ingots to that cock sucker!"

The group stood in silence for a moment.

"If this is going to work in anyway, we need to scout out their staging area and find out what we're dealing with," Alex said and finally voiced his opinion.

"And why would we do that?" Conrad asked in a snotty tone.

"We need to know how many Accaren mercenaries Trails has on the ground," Alex retorted, "if the number of slaves talked about is accurate, my guess is at least two hundred."

Ferrell looked down at the holo-map in deep concentration.

"Alright, scout it out and report back," he commanded to both Alex and Cameron.

"We will comm in when we have more information," Alex replied.

Cameron gave a slight nod of her head before she turned and followed her mentor. They walked off the command deck, through the sliding blast doors and into the spacious corridor. As they strolled, Cameron noticed dozens of Tuskerons. They were busy carrying supplies and weapons. Others were busy repairing and maintaining the warship.

The pair walked in silence. Halfway to the hangar bay, Cameron looked up and realized Alex was mumbling to himself.

"What's wrong?" she asked.

Alex looked down at her with a smile.

"It's nothing, but I still have to say it. Screw Conrad Masters. How an incompetent boy gained the title of Slave Lord I will never know," he replied.

"He had his father murdered," Cameron voiced the rumor.

"But who pulled the trigger?" Alex questioned.

"My question, why hasn't someone put an energy bolt in Conrad yet?" Cameron asked.

Alex laughed out loud at the comment.

"It's just a cruel fate of the universe," Alex said with a chuckle.

They continued down the hallway until they reached a large landing bay. It was full of shuttles, dropships, and other armaments. Cameron looked down at the grates beneath her feet. She saw a second landing bay of equal size and held two-dozen slave barges. They were in a straight line and stretched the entire length of the lower landing bay.

Cameron and Alex weaved through the maze of transports and dropships, until they reached their ride. They came to a stop in front of an old, beat up Ranger shuttle. It was black with sloping sides and narrow triangle shaped wings.

Alex climbed up on the vessel and opened the hatch which was located on the left.

"So, we're riding in that ancient piece of shit?" Cameron asked with hesitation.

Alex turned back and gazed down at his pupil.

"Yes, we are," he replied with a smile, "but this piece of shit has a full cloaking system, compared to the other pieces of shit laying around the landing bay. Unless you want to get shot down?"

"No thank you," Cameron replied feeling slightly embarrassed after his simplistic reasoning.

Cameron climbed onto the wing and followed Alex into the vessel. The shuttle was cramped with a small cargo hold and two seats. Cameron moved forward and took her station at the co-pilot's chair. To her right, Cameron noticed lettering engraved on the wall. Upon closer inspection she translated the lettering as Accaren and roughly said `Sparrow' in basic.

"What's a Sparrow?" Cameron asked her mentor and helped prep the ship for launch.

"Sparrow?" Alex clarified.

"Correct," Cameron stated.

Alex looked down at the floor grate as he tried to recall the word.

"A sparrow is a small bird from Old Earth. They stowed away when the Humans left their former home and came to Known-Space," Alex explained, "I've only seen one here, but you find a lot of them in the Void."

Cameron instantly stopped what she was doing and looked over at him with surprise.

"You've been to the Void?" Cameron questioned.

The Void was a desolate part of the universe which served as a natural barrier between Known-Space and the Orion-Cluster. From what Cameron had heard over the years, it was filled with solar storms, wormholes, and dark matter pockets. Endless loops in space which stranded countless ships in an inescapable maze.

A place of terror and death.

If you don't have it memorized, don't go in. Cameron remembered a smuggler saying a year back.

In all the years Cameron had known Alex, she had never heard him mention a journey to the border of the unknown.

"A few times, what are the core power levels at?" Alex replied vaguely and changed the subject.

"Power levels are normal," Cameron quickly stated, "but the Draith control ninety percent of the entrance to the Void?" Cameron thought out loud, "while the Valari control the other."

She saw Alex in her peripheral vision. He glanced over at her and then back at the controls.

"Diagnostic check on cloak?" Alex confirmed and interrupted her thoughts once again.

"Clean," Cameron replied without hesitation.

"Frequency?"

"Eighty-four, seventy-two, fifty-three," Cameron spouted back quite proud at her own efficiency.

Cameron took off her coat, crossed her arms and leaned back deep in thought.

"You wouldn't have gone with Ferrell, this would have been during your time with the Ranger Empire," she redirected again.

"Cameron Lynn Summers."

Her back straightened and Cameron sat up at the sound of her full name being said. She gazed back at her mentor with a crooked smile.

"Do you have a specific question?" he asked.

"Why were you in the Void?" Cameron asked with endless intrigue at the subject.

Alex sat silent at her direct question. He pressed a few buttons on the control panel and started the engines. The shuttle shook for a moment before it lifted off the deck plates.

"You know how much I love the Void and you always say it's good for me to learn about things that could affect Ferrell. This would be for my strategic training," Cameron explained with a playful smile.

"Well played Cammy," Alex said and complemented Cameron on her vocal tactics.

Alex carefully navigated the small craft through the maze of ships and flew out of the hanger bay at moderate speed.

"Back when I was sixteen, the Ranger High Council assigned me to a long range six-unit commando team. Now remember twenty years ago no one knew who the Draith were. After I had been assigned to my team, we were summoned before the Ranger Council," Alex explained, "they informed us of a race that lived in the Void. No one from the military had seen these beings only reports from the outer colonies. So, they sent us into the Void to investigate."

Once they were far enough from the fleet, Alex made the jump to subspace.

"What happened next?" Cameron asked with breathless anticipation.

Alex just smiled at her excitement.

"We discovered true evil, and our people's extinction," he replied in a darkened tone.

Cameron could see the pain in his expression as Alex recalled the memories.

"We had only been in the Void for a few days before they found us. Like the Rangers, the Draith had limited contact with our people, and in our first meeting they mistook us for Humans. Our biggest mistake was proving them wrong," Alex said with regret in his voice.

"To this day I don't know why they reacted the way they did. Once they realized we were ability-based, there was nothing we could say or do to stop their unyielding hatred of us. After that, I spent over a year in hell before I was able to escape," he finished.

"Did the Draith invade Known-Space just out of hatred for the Ranger race?" Cameron asked.

Alex took a moment to ponder the question.

"I've always suspected that was part of it, but in my experience that was not the true reason," Alex replied.

Cameron sat at the edge of her seat, intrigued by the former Ranger Captain.

"Funny thing about the Draith invasion. Most individuals believe the Draith invaded Known-Space. They were actually pushed out of the Void."

His answer caught Cameron by surprise. Everything she had learned. Not only in the Ranger schools on Zail, but the Human schools on Agron also said it was because of the Rangers. Even the extra non-standard education she received on Camus failed to mention any other reason for the Draith invasion.

"But—"

"I know what you've been told, but the Ranger High Council buried the truth. They locked my report away and lied about the reality. They can't accept there are beings stronger and bolder than them," Alex said and cut her off.

It was Cameron's turn to ponder his phrasing.

"I don't understand," she admitted.

"I'm sure in your time around Rangers you've heard the term Guardian or Fallen?" Alex inquired.

He was correct. Cameron had heard the term more than once from her parents before their death on Rydon.

"Yes. The Humans call them angels and demons, but those are just stories. No one has any proof of their existence," Cameron countered.

She stopped, crossed her arms and stared at through the front window. Alex chuckled and waited.

"No way," Cameron exclaimed and turned back, "So, your telling me you've seen an angel?"

"After I escaped the Draith, I was captured by the Xan who took me to the Demonic Princess, and her horde a Reapers," Alex explained, "they took us to a giant ship or as I like to refer to it...hell."

Cameron was floored by his statement. She sat there for a moment as her mind tried its best to come to terms with the shocking news.

"What are they like?" Cameron asked and tried to imagine the demonic beings.

"They are as beautiful as they are terrifying. Flawless skin, jet-black wings. They are strong, spiteful and ruthless," Alex stopped almost mid-sentence.

Cameron could tell that he was shifting through memories.

"I remember sitting in a cell when a beautiful woman walked up, black hair with dark piercing eyes. They were black with almost a reddish tint. Her wings were folded and concealed under her jacket. From her appearance I would have sworn she was Human. She looked nineteen but was in fact thousands of years old," Alex recalled, "she was sweet, flirtatious, but let me tell you Cammy she was screwed up. She liked playing games, and each one was even more twisted then the last."

Cameron could tell the memory of the ordeal still bothered him.

"What was her name?" Cameron asked, her mind still overflowing with questions.

"Elyzabeth, Princess of the Void," Alex replied.

Cameron cocked her head to the side. She was also surprised by the demon's name.

So, she did mean a literal demon. Cameron thought as her memories went back to her and Shelby's conversation.

"I remember a strange Human in the cell next to me, gods what was his name," Alex said and snapped his fingers, "Elyjah. Elyjah Morgan. Yeah let me tell you, Elyzabeth had a truly unhealthy obsession with that poor kid."

Alex turned back to the ships controls and double checked the readings.

"What happened next?" Cameron asked after what felt like an eternity, but her mentor merely laughed.

"Can't tell you the whole thing now," he replied with a smile, "we need more alcohol for that, way more."

* * *

It was a short jump to Daigys. Lights flashed on the overhead terminal and indicated they had reached their destination.

"Here we go," Alex said in a dry unenthusiastic tone.

The puddle-jumper jolted sharply as they entered the system. Cameron stretched out her hand and activated the cloak.

"We're like ghosts." Cameron said with a smirk.

"Sensor readings?" Alex asked and checked her focus.

"Looks like five Accaren cruisers, and two marauders," Cameron replied.

"We'll take heavy losses from their cluster missiles. Other than that, should be a quick in and out," Alex commented.

He piloted the small craft undetected through the maze of patrolling Accarens. They passed through the atmosphere and down to the swamps of Daigys. The planet was covered by murky bogs with small islands. The second half of the planet was covered in lush grassy plains which were naturally higher in elevation. This created a natural border separating them.

Cameron looked out the window and saw narrow, winding pathways. They spread across the landscape, zig-zagging around small islands.

"I'm liking there," Alex said and pointed to a small piece of land.

He set the ship down on a small island and carefully steered around the massive trees.

"According to our sensors, we have a large group of lifeforms a half a click northwest," Cameron said after the rough landing.

"So far so good kid," Alex said referring to her directly.

She tilted her head in confusion. She knew something was up, but Alex had not revealed his hidden test. A Ranger practice he was accustomed to.

"Today is your final test, Cammy," Alex said to her delight.

"I am not only going to grade you by Ferrell's standards, but also that of Auctus Battle Academy," he continued, "if you were with our people you would be promoted to lieutenant and would be sent to command training."

"Understood," Cameron replied with a confident nod.

They stood up and made their way back into the small cargo bay. Alex popped the hatch and the smell of the stagnant water filled the cabin.

"Oh yuck," Cameron said nauseated by the odor.

"Wait until you're neck deep in it and it's coming in your mouth," Alex said with a chuckle.

He knew she hated `playing in the mud' as he called it. Alex stepped in front of her and exited the vessel. He stepped into the knee-high pool and proceeded to wade deeper into the murky water. She gave out a slight gasp as the ice-cold water soaked through her pants and shirt. Alex looked back with surprise at her lack of silence.

"It's damn cold," Cameron whispered.

Alex smiled in response. He stepped deeper into the swamp and soon it was up to his waist. Cameron promptly followed. She gritted her teeth as the water rose to her shoulders. In some areas she was forced to tread water and almost had to swim to keep up with Alex.

After twenty minutes of rough terrain, they finally reached the border of the swamp.

Beyond the shore was a rock face. It seemed to be comprised of boulders with a dirt foundation. It was forty meters in height and appeared a rough climb. Cameron pulled herself onto the bank and immediately brushed the debris that had stuck to her skin.

Alex wasted little time and started scaling the rock face. Cameron rung out her ponytail and followed. She chose her footing with care as she made her way up. Hearing footsteps they instantly stopped and looked down at the ground below. Through the foliage they could see shades of blue.

Cameron's heart jumped into her throat at the sight of the Accaren Knight. He appeared to be patrolling the border of the slave camp. He stealthily moved through the water and stopped directly below them at the base of the rock face. Cameron looked up at Alex who held his index finger to his lips.

Cameron knew it was a reminder about the Accaren's native armor. It had a full HUD, also equipped with a pin-point sound grid. This allowed the Accaren to pick up the slightest noise, even a whisper. Accaren armor was at the top of the food chain in a galaxy of armor. If he saw them, they would have one chance before he would be able to contact the main base.

The Accaren turned and started back on his patrol. Seeing the threat had passed, Alex powered down his energy-hammer. This almost silent noise stirred the Accaren Knight. He whipped around with his energy-pistol drawn. A bright flash emanated as the Knight pulled the trigger.

Alex stretched out his hand and created an energy barrier in front of he and Cameron. The bolt pounded against the barrier, centimeters away from his face. Near the Energy-Caster's skull. The Accaren extended his shield but Cameron was ready. She used her ability to lift the Knight and slammed him into the earth.

Alex activated his fourth ascension and created an impenetrable bubble around the Knight. Without so much as a glance, Alex powered up the energy-hammer and leapt from the rock face. Within a split second, Alex dropped the shield and launched his level five ability into the helmet of the Accaren.

In the same second Cameron extended her hand and used her ascension to catch Alex before he fell to his death. Cameron took a deep breath.

Her heart raced while Alex remained motionless. He hung about twelve centimeters from the ground with his hands on either side. She set him down gently and turned her attention back to the Accaren.

Although Alex hit him with everything he had at close range, the Accaren's helmet was unmarred.

"I liquified his brain," Alex said in a quiet tone.

He sounded confident, almost as if he spoke from personal experience.

"Hey Cammy, can you give me a lift?" he continued with a smirk.

Cameron gave him a crooked smile in return and lifted her mentor up to the top. It took her about fifteen minutes, but Cameron finally joined him. She looked over and saw Alex. He was laying prone and took cover behind two decent sized rocks. Cameron kept low and crawled up next to him.

She reached back and pulled out a small pair of field-glasses. She focused her eyes and stared out at the beautiful plains. Large valleys stretched for miles with the occasional patch of trees. The slave camps spread across the valley. Upon closer inspection Cameron saw every variety of alien she could think of. Human, Accaren, Tuskeron, and more. Over ten-thousand by her estimation. On the outskirts she saw Alex's prior concern. There were hundreds of Accarens, Knights and Flight-Techs guarded the slaves and perimeter of the staging area.

Alex pulled out his comm and held it to his mouth.

"James," he said quietly into the device.

"I read you," Ferrell replied after a second.

"Well, the space is the easy part. Accaren cruisers and marauders," Alex said and gave Ferrell his tactical assessment.

"And the ground?" the Slave Lord replied.

"The ground is a different matter. By my count we're looking at ten to twelve thousand slaves. There's around five hundred Accaren Knights and roughly two hundred and fifty Flight-Techs."

There was a pause on Ferrell's end of the line. Mumbling could be heard as he gave the information to Maglar and Conrad.

"What's your assessment?" Ferrell asked.

"We can win it, but we'll take heavy losses. My guess is three to one in Trails' favor."

Five or six seconds passed as Ferrell did the math.

"Good work. We'll take it from here," Ferrell stated.

The line went dead, and Alex hooked the device back onto his belt.

"So, what's next?" Cameron whispered.

Alex just smiled.

"Our part is done, Cammy. Now we just get to sit and watch the show," Alex replied in a calm tone.

"We won't be participating in the raid?" Cameron asked with surprise.

"Nope. We are too valuable to be risked on an attack of this scale."

"But you and I could cut our losses in half, "Cameron debated.

"Remember Cameron, Accarens hate our people even more then the Draith. As soon as we use our abilities, every one of those spite filled bastards would target us," Alex replied.

Cameron could hear the dislike of the Accarens in his voice. In less than an hour, flashes filled the evening sky. Alarms sounded in the camp and alerted the Accarens of the incoming danger.

"There goes Trails' fleet," Alex whispered.

He pointed at multiple flashes in the skies above. Soon after, Cameron saw hundreds of black dots appear on the horizon. As they came closer, she could see the distinctive markings of Tuskeron dropships. They were loaded to the max – carrying over fourteen hundred Tuskerons.

The dropships closed on the camp with marvelous speed. The Knights took up defensive position and extended their shields. The Flight-Tech's took to the air and set course for the incoming Tuskerons.

Both sides opened fire with hundreds of energy missiles and cannons. Orange energy bursts flashed from the Accaren shields. The Flight-Techs fired barrages of cluster-missiles. The missiles impacted the dropship's shields with shades of blue and silver.

Finally, in range, the dropships encircled the camp and started landing troops. Cameron was amazed, even though the Tuskerons were three times the size. For every Accaren killed at least two Tuskerons were cut down in return.

As the battle continued Ferrell's strategy became clear. He did not care about loss of life and overwhelmed the Accarens with sheer numbers.

Within thirty minutes the raid had concluded. There were nearly a thousand dead, Tuskerons and Accarens alike.

Alex and Cameron took to their feet and made their way down to the remnants of the battlefield. The dead were being stacked like firewood with little care given to their burial. By the time they walked across the grassy field there were three Tuskeron warships overhead. The rumble of their engines vibrated the ground. As they reached their ride, Cameron gave one final look back. Hundreds of slave barges set course from the warships.

Alex and Cameron took their seats in the dropship. Seconds later, the hatch sealed, and the engines fired up with a boom. The vessel lifted off the ground and set course for the Tuskeron Flagship.

After a five-minute ride, the dropship set down in the once full hanger bay. They exited the vessel in silence and made their way to the command deck.

As they rounded the final corner, Cameron heard raised voices. Fearing something was wrong, their pace quickened and turned in to a dead run.

Cameron and Alex sprinted onto the command deck only to see Conrad jumping around in excitement and held a champagne bottle. He looked up at the ceiling and poured the alcohol into his mouth. The champagne overflowed and covered his face and shirt. Cameron's eyes scanned the room. She searched for Ferrell who she figured would be disgusted by the man's actions, but to her amazement Ferrell was on the other side of the bridge with a drink of his own. Even more shocking, he was laughing at Conrad's childish behavior.

"We're filthy rich!" Conrad yelled out at the top of his lungs.

"Damn right!" Ferrell laughed and raised his glass in response.

Alex and Cameron were floored by Ferrell's newly found joy.

"And the best part, we stole it all from that asshat Colin Trails," Ferrell spouted.

He turned to the doorway and saw the Rangers both standing in silence.

"Welcome back my friends!" Ferrell yelled over at them.

He picked up a second glass and walked over. Ferrell handed the newly poured drink to Alex.

"Thank you," Alex replied.

Their glasses made a soft ping as they toasted their success and victory.

"How bad were our losses?" Alex asked.

Ferrell waved away his concern.

"It doesn't matter with the profits we made," he replied and ignored the sacrifice of hundreds of Tuskerons.

"Do you know what we should do?" Ferrell said and walked back to the center of the bridge, "we should celebrate by going to the nicest casino on Oc'tal'ia."

"Hell yeah, some gambling and parafeks. I'm down," Conrad whined.

Cameron rolled her eyes in response to his comment. It was a practice the Ranger was accustomed to with her face generally being covered.

"It's decided, I'll send the fleet back to Camus and we will be at Oc'tal'ia in a few hours," Ferrell proclaimed.

Cameron nodded her head in compliance. She turned to leave but did not hear Alex beside her. She looked back and saw him standing in the doorway.

"Go on kid," he said with a motion of his hand.

Cameron nodded again and continued to her quarters. She walked through the massive five-meter-high ceiling corridor and passed over two dozen Tuskerons. They simply looked down and continued with their work. She looped around and went down two levels to the crew quarters on the vessel.

Almost there, Cameron thought to herself.

Her entire thought process since landing on Daigys was getting back to the ship and washing the slime and muck off her skin and hair. She stopped at her door for a few seconds before entering. It swung inward to the narrow yet tall room. Cameron put her hands on the bed and took a deep breath.

She shook her head and walked into the bathroom. The Telekinetic turned on the rain like shower and allowed the water to warm. Cameron peeled off her filth ridden clothes and gazed into the mirror.

For the briefest of moments, she saw a reflection of a thirteen-year-old girl. Terrified and alone. She saw not only herself, but also the world she had been thrown into. Her young innocence which had been stolen by Ferrell, Alex, and so many others. The mirror started to fog, and the image reverted to its original form.

"Happy birthday, Cammy," she said to the fading reflection.

Cameron turned and stepped into the steamy shower. The water rushed over her tanned skin and turned black as it washed the mud and grass off her. It was not that her birthday was a big celebration. In fact, Alex was the only one who cared, but this year he had not said anything.

He must have been thinking about the raid, Cameron thought to herself, i*s this where my life has gone? Five years as the protector of piss and shit.*

She had not seen her Grandfather in over two years, and sadly had learned to accept his absence. Some days she did not even know if he were alive, but the seventeen-year-old kept faith she would see her last surviving family again.

Cameron finished washing and gave herself one final rinse. She exited the shower, pulled a white over-sized towel off the rack and dried off her body. She finished with her hair and wrapped the towel around her.

She made her way back into the bedroom and started dressing.

Cameron had just put on her pants when she heard a knock at the door. She quickly threw on a tank top, picked up her hairbrush and opened the door. She was pleasantly surprised to see Alex, white t-shirt, blue jeans and short blond hair.

"Hey kid," he said with a warm smile, "we'll be at Oc'tal'ia in the next few hours."

Cameron motioned with her hand and let him in. Alex shut the door upon entry as Cameron made her way over to the bed. She took a seat on the firm mattress and continued brushing her hair.

"Happy birthday, Cameron," Alex said.

He pulled out a small box, walked forward and handed it to her. Cameron opened it slowly and saw a Ranger graduation medal.

"Alex, this is yours," Cameron stuttered.

"Not anymore. You earned it Cammy," he replied with a warm smile.

Alex knelt in front of her. He removed the red, blue and gold pendant and pinned it on her shirt.

"Thank you," the teen Ranger exclaimed.

"You're welcome."

Alex stood back up. He put his hands in his pockets and stared down at the floor. Cameron could tell something was on his mind, but it was not like him to be anything other than blunt.

"Cameron, I want to tell you how proud of you I am. In the years I've known you, I've watched you grow into a strong, beautiful Ranger. You have passed every expectation, project or test I've ever had, and I would not be here if not for you."

"Alex—" Cameron said and tried not to get choked up.

"You are the daughter I always wanted, but never had," he finished.

A tear rolled down her cheek at his words.

"Alex, that means the world to me," she replied with a warm smile.

A second tear rolled down, but Alex extended his hand and wiped it from her face.

"Get some rest kid, I'll see you in a few hours," Alex said.

He turned and stepped through the door.

"Goodnight," she replied.

Alone once again, Cameron crawled under the sheets. She took off the medal and held it to her chest.

"Thank you. Thank you for always being there," Cameron said quietly.

She closed her eyes and soon fell fast asleep.

* * *

Cameron's eyes flashed open and she gasped at the sound of a loud knock on her door. It was panicked and rapid.

"Cameron, were under attack!" Alex's voice boomed.

Adrenaline flooded her bloodstream to the point that she was shaking and cold.

"Shit!" Cameron exclaimed and fell out of bed.

She scrambled on all fours for her boots, cargo pants and coat. With little more than her messed hair, tank top and boy shorts Cameron rushed out the door bare foot and held her gear. She slammed the door and turned around to see Alex leaning against the bulkhead. Cameron looked from side to side, but the halls were empty. No alarms with no troops preparing for battle. Cameron looked up at Alex for clarification. He stood up and put his hands at his sides.

"Oldest graduation prank in the book," Alex said with a chuckle.

"Dick..." Cameron muttered in an annoyed tone.

"Don't be grumpy Cammy, at least you had some clothes on," he said with a laugh.

Cameron gave a wide-eyed look of disbelief.

"Yep," Alex confirmed with a nod, "and I was not alone. I'll have to tell you that story sometime."

"I'm going to go change," Cameron said with a laugh.

A few moments later she returned waring her second favorite outfit. White shirt, with jeans and combat boots. Her brown leather blazer was thrown over her shoulder. She had cleaned up her appearance and brushed her long brown hair behind her ears.

Cameron put on her jacket and signaled her readiness. She followed her mentor down the hallways and into the hanger bay. They made their way across the hanger and walked up the stairs into Ferrell's personal transport.

The shuttle took off and was followed closely by two Tuskeron dropships. Their protection for the descent to the planet below.

Cameron did what she could to tame her hair as her brown eyes stayed fixed on the window. Her vision was locked on the awe-inspiring sight of Oc'tal'ia's enormous skyscrapers. Each one unique in its own design. The planet was a game world, bright and colorful. It had every pleasure in Known-Space in one spot and was considered the jewel of the Ninth Faction.

What do you think happens when you base a society on slavery? Cameron thought to herself, *you get every sick and twisted pleasure you can imagine. Like Zootalia.*

The vessel set down on a large landing pad attached to the casino. Cameron took a moment to take one last view at the city. She stood up and followed Alex and Ferrell off the ship. They were met by two dozen Tuskeron guards who escorted them into the casino.

There were tables scattered around the bar with a hexagon cage in the center of the room. There was a large group standing and howling as a fight progressed. In the current match two massive rhino-bred Tuskerons were trading blow for blow. The first landed a heavy punch. The other rhino's head whipped to the side as the beast fell with a crash. The second hybrid made it back to his feet, charged forward and lifted its opponent. The rhino roared out and threw the hybrid to the ground.

The mob roared at what appeared to be an unexpected victory.

"James!" Conrad's whine sounded from a private booth off to the left.

They walked over and joined the fellow Slave Lord. There was a table with padded chairs around it. Ferrell sat on the opposite side with Alex and Cameron behind him.

Conrad sat comfortably on his side of the table, drink in hand with two female Accarens standing behind him. Cameron could tell they were Accaren by orange hexagon tattoos under their eyes.

"Allow me to introduce Shaya and Mika, two of my favorite personal slaves."

Cameron looked over the Accarens. Both females seemed oddly similar with matching corn rows and overall athletic builds. They were identical with one exception, Shaya wore yellow, while Mika had green coloring.

"Oh, did I mention they are twins, and have fantastic personalities," Conrad smirked.

"No, you did not," Ferrell commented.

"Drinks!" Conrad commanded.

"Cameron, would you mind?" Alex asked.

"I'm on it," she replied.

As Cameron walked away both Accarens glared in her direction with anger and hatred. She did not know how, but Cameron had the impression they knew she was a Ranger. It was impossible, but it was the only thing she could think of. Cameron walked around the tables and up to the bar. She looked for the bar tender, but he was helping other customers. Cameron leaned against the bar counter and waited patiently to be served.

"So, you've met the Savior of Brighton?" she heard a man next to her ask his companion.

Cameron had heard the title more than once in years past. Its owner was that of Kyle Marcus Knight, A young Ranger Fire-Caster who survived the destruction of Rydon. In years past, Kyle had battled Draith and Ninth Faction forces alike. His most famous victory was that of Brighton, of what the Humans called the Battle of Brothers.

I wonder what he's like, she pondered.

"What can I get you, little lady?" the bartender asked and snapped her mind back to the present.

"I need to open a tab for James Ferrell. We'll start with a double shot of Human whisky, neat. Two glasses of twenty-five-year-old single malt scotch, neat, and a Shirley Temple please," Cameron said in a professional and polite tone.

"Right away sweetie," he replied promptly.

Cameron turned away from the bar and walked back in the direction of the group. As she approached, Cameron saw Conrad point at her and ask Ferrell a question. She was not sure what they were saying but Alex had a disgusted look on his face.

"So, you've never?" Conrad asked.

"No Conrad," Ferrell replied as if he thought it was a stupid question.

"Your loss," Conrad said in almost a depressed tone.

Cameron did not know what they were talking about and she was sure she did not want to. A waitress dropped off their drinks. Ferrell and Conrad tipped her before she sauntered off.

"So how about a wager to pass the time?" Conrad asked and took a swig off his drink.

"Is it that time already, Conrad?" Ferrell asked and looked down at an imaginary watch.

"Very funny, James. I was thinking of a friendly sparring match," Conrad whined in response.

"I'll fight you," Alex interjected with a laugh.

Conrad frowned back at him. He did not respond and turned his attention back to Ferrell.

"You take pride in your slave control, combat and overall training, correct?" Conrad asked.

"You're correct," Ferrell replied.

"How about we pit our personal slaves in the hexagon, Shaya verses Cameron?" Conrad queried.

Ferrell stared out into space as he considered the bet.

"What's the purse?" Ferrell asked.

"One thousand Accaren slaves," Conrad stated.

"So low?" Ferrell replied.

Conrad was taken aback by the Slave Lords response.

"One round or until knock out for three thousand Accaren slaves," Ferrell countered.

It turned Cameron's stomach at the thought of being wagered for slaves, but in the end that was the sad reality of the cards she had been dealt.

"I could accept those terms," Conrad replied.

Both men shook hands and motioned for Shaya and Cameron to take position. The Accaren wasted no time and moved in the direction of the hexagon. Alex and Cameron made their way to the opposite side and stood a meter from the entrance.

Cameron weaved and dodged back and forth as she warmed up. Alex leaned forward and gained her attention. He put his hands firmly on her shoulders and leaned close.

"You've trained for this. You know both Accaren martial-art forms. Just make sure to watch out for grapples," Alex said firmly, "and keep your guard up."

"I haven't dropped my left in months," Cameron playfully retorted.

"Keep telling yourself that," Alex teased, "now go kick her ass.'

Cameron gave him a confident nod, handed over her jacket and stepped into the hexagon. A crowd had already assembled and started placing bets on the match. Shaya and Cameron stepped forward, ready to fight.

"Begin!" Conrad commanded.

Both females started circling one another. Being an Accaren, Shaya had advantages. She not only had denser muscles, but also a heavier build and was a few centimeters taller than Cameron. The Ranger kept her hands around the lower half of her face as she continued to step from side to side.

Shaya was first to strike. She threw a jab which Cameron deflected. The Accaren struck again, but just as before the Ranger blocked the attack. Becoming frustrated, Shaya threw a right hook. This was the opportunity Cameron had been waiting for. She ducked under the heavy attack and moved to the left. She balled up her left fist and countered with a square hit to Shaya's ribs.

The Accaren yelled out in pain. Cameron could hear at least two ribs break from the strike. Cameron shifted her body and swung with a right hook. Still recovering, the Telekinetic's attack was unchallenged. Her fist collided with Shaya's mouth and nose. The crowd roared as blood splattered across the mat. Cameron continued forward and kicked, but Shaya was one step ahead of her.

The Accaren gripped her leg. Cameron felt herself lift into the air, and then rapidly descend. Her head slammed into the mat, and for a moment she saw stars. Shaya mounted the Ranger and started swinging. Cameron immediately brought her hands up in defense from the continued attacks but no matter what she did, the Accaren's punches broke through.

Her eyes swelled, and Cameron had the taste of blood in her mouth. She used what strength she had left and secured Shaya's right arm by pulling herself up. The Accaren continued to hit Cameron's back over and over with her free hand.

Cameron locked the Accaren's arm in place. She leaned back, and with one fluid motion shifted her bodyweight and struck the Accaren with her elbow. Shaya rolled to the side and Cameron found herself on top. The Telekinetic countered with another elbow and cut Shaya's face. Cameron repeated the move and started wailing on her.

The Accaren started to lose consciousness. Cameron took hold of her shirt, lifted Shaya's head off the ground and uppercut her opponent. Shaya's head slammed against the mat, out cold from the blow.

The crowd roared at the top of their lungs as Cameron stood up slowly.

"Yeah!" she screamed and ignited the crowd even more.

Alex made his way into the hexagon, he put a towel over Cameron and helped her out.

"Good fight, kid!" Alex yelled over the noise of the howling mob.

Cameron felt sick. She was not sure if it was the adrenaline, her injuries, or the ear-piercing sounds of the crowd.

"I need some air!" she yelled up at Alex.

He escorted her outside the bar and made their way to an empty landing pad. The Rangers were followed by Sargus and three additional guards. Each one held an assault-rifle. As soon as they made it outside, Cameron ran to the edge of the platform and started puking. Alex made his way over and knelt beside her.

"It's okay, it's just the adrenaline," Alex said, and put his hand on her back.

"I did it," she said in shock.

"Yes, you did, Cameron," Alex replied with a smile.

Cameron took to her feet and used the towel to wipe her face and hands. After a few moments she started to feel more like herself.

"How bad do I look?" she asked tentatively and touched her cut lip.

"Like you just beat the shit out of an Accaren," Alex said with a chuckle.

"Thanks Alex," she replied and playfully punched him in the arm.

"I have a surprise for you Cameron. This is not only for everything you did tonight, but also a gift for your loyal service. Ferrell and I are giving you one free night," Alex said, to Cameron's delight.

"You can go anywhere or do anything on this planet you want. Just be home by morning," he explained.

This was something Cameron had always dreamed of. The true freedom that she craved.

"Hell yeah!" she exclaimed and put her fists in the air.

Alex just laughed.

"Glad you approve," he replied.

Cameron froze and put her hands at her sides.

"What's wrong?" Alex asked and noticed her concern.

"Alex how far up are we?" she inquired.

"Eight hundred to a thousand meters," he quickly replied.

"I can feel the aura of—"

The platform rumbled, and a small Human transport rose into view.

"Form up!" Alex commanded and raised his shield in defense.

Before the Tuskerons could react, the transport opened fire with a line of energy-bolts. The fire took out two of the four guards. The ship redirected its fire to Alex and pounded against the barrier.

"It's Logan Masters!" Cameron yelled and recognized the aura of the former Human commando they had ran into a few years back.

A shot sounded, and a flash could be seen from the neighboring building. A split second later an energy bolt took out the third guard. This left Sargus, Alex and Cameron.

"Sniper!" Cameron called out.

Sargus turned and stayed in front of the Rangers. He lifted his rifle and returned fire while Alex maintained the shield.

"Cameron, deal with the ship!" Alex commanded.

She could tell from the sound of his voice he was losing control of the barrier. Cameron moved to the side and used her abilities to take hold of the ship. Another shot sounded and Sargus roared out in pain. The rhino stumbled back and gripped his shoulder.

"Hammer!" Alex yelled, and fired his fifth ascension in the direction of the sniper. Moments later dust flew up around the location.

Cameron shifted her arms downward and threw the vessel into the side of the building. She turned back to Alex with a look of success. He returned her gaze with fear and stared down at her chest. Cameron looked down and saw a red dot.

"Cameron!" Alex yelled and stepped into the sniper's line of sight.

A shot rang out, the worst sound of her life.

Before she knew what happened, Alex fell on top of her and threw them both to the metal pad.

Sargus recovered and stepped in front of them. Cameron looked over at Alex and gasped out at the sight. The HT-54 sniper round had nearly blown a hole through his chest. Blood pooled on the pavement and he gasped for air. His eyes locked with hers.

"Alex!" Cameron screamed and rushed to his aid.

She put his head in her lap and gripped his hand tightly.

"Call a medic!" she screamed at Sargus.

"Looks like I'm not going to be able to tell you the rest of that story," he said with a cough, "just know Elijah was nuts and Elyzabeth was a bitch."

Tears swelled in her eyes and soon poured down her cheeks.

"No, no," Cameron kept repeating in hopeless desperation, "you can't leave me, you promised."

Alex put his hand on her cheek.

"You promised you would always protect me!"

"I love you, kid—" Alex said before life fled him.

Alex Sheridan was dead.

In that moment Cameron felt her heart sink and a part of her world collapse.

"Alex!" she screamed.

Cameron held him close, breathless and without thought. Tears poured down her cheeks as she gazed upon the pale reflection of her mentor and best friend. Cameron felt physical pain and shook as she started to hyperventilate. Her eyes were red, and her cheeks were stained. Cameron quivered with increasing rage. Her fists tightened and she grit her teeth. Soon after, the pain turned into a quest for vengeance.

"Sniper is retreating," Sargus yelled and yanked her mind back to the present.

Cameron gently laid Alex down and took to her feet. Cameron peered over at the adjacent building to see a black and gray figure rappel down the face. Her pain turned to hatred and had one singular goal.

"I want a two-kilometer lockdown on the perimeter," Cameron commanded.

Without another word she was on the hunt. Cameron turned and sprinted forward. Without any hesitation she leapt off the ledge of the platform. While free falling, Cameron kept her eyes locked on the white figure. As she approached the ground, Cameron put her hands to the side and slowed her descent. Her boots hit the ground and she took off in a dead sprint with one target in mind.

"I'll kill her for what she did," Cameron said in hatred.

Her tone was dark, and she knew what she needed to do. Cameron did not have her coat but cared little and sprinted in her white blood-stained shirt.

She made two sharp turns and was soon behind her target. Cameron stretched forth her hand and took hold of the Human commando with her ascension. She threw her arm to the side and hurled the Human into the side of the building, but she did not stop there. Cameron slammed the commando time and time again into the pavement until she heard a crack.

Cameron held her target above, prepared to inflict more damage. The commando's armor was broken. Chest plate was cracked, and her helmet had come off.

"Who are you?" Cameron yelled at the black-haired woman.

"Lieutenant Jade Diez," she coughed.

"Why did you do it?" Cameron screamed, "he was a kind Ranger. He was my friend."

"No! He was a damned traitor who butchered countless innocent lives," Jade snapped back, "just like you."

Cameron hurled the battered woman to the ground in anger. Jade rolled across the pavement and came to a stop a few meters from the Telekinetic. Cameron reached out with her hand and pulled Jade back toward her. The young Ranger stepped forward in anger and pressed her boot against Jade's throat.

"I don't care," Cameron sneered in a cold tone, "he was my friend and you took him away from me."

"I did it for Logan…you most likely killed him when you destroyed his ship. He's a lucky man and I wouldn't bet against him," Jade replied and coughed up a mouthful of blood.

"So that's it?" the Ranger scoffed, "you did it for a man who couldn't let go of the past?"

"No, I killed him as a statement for Human superiority and vengeance," Jade hissed.

"I'll show you vengeance," Cameron replied with hatred.

Cameron used her telekinetic powers and hurled Jade across the pavement.

"True vengeance," she cried out, "I'm not going to kill you. I'm taking you back to James Ferrell and see what he wants to say. I'm sure he will have a bunch of questions for you."

Their attention was stolen by the sight of two Tuskeron dropships. They flew down and landed a few meters away from Cameron and Jade. The door opened and Sargus stood inside.

"Ferrell commands us to leave," the rhino roared.

"Secure the Human," Cameron yelled to the second dropship.

A pair of Tuskerons repelled down and took custody of Jade.

"Take her back to Camus under heavy guard," the Ranger commanded.

The Tuskerons complied with her orders and drug Jade kicking and screaming into the dropship. Cameron turned and entered the first vessel.

"What now?" Cameron questioned.

"Vau'Tir, Syprus, and Me'er are under attack by Colin Trails. Ferrell is taking us back to Camus," Sargus replied.

"Any sign of Logan Masters?" she questioned as the door sealed.

"Nothing," Sargus replied.

"No remains?" she pressed.

"Nothing," the Tuskeron repeated.

Cameron screamed out in agony. The other Tuskerons glanced over but remained silent. Her voice was filled with pain and loss. She had no idea what to do. How she was going to survive the next day. Soon her emotions overtook the teen Ranger and tears filled her brown eyes. She covered her face and sobbed for the loss of Alex Sheridan.

INTO THE FIRE

It had been two days since the nightmare on Oc'tal'ia. Since the death of Alex Sheridan and Jades capture. Ferrell and Cameron stood just outside the fortress, dressed in attire with Alex's headstone a few meters in front of them. Cameron had not said a word, and merely kept her eyes fixed on his name.

"We are here to remember our fallen brothers and sisters," Cameron said and recited the Ranger remembrance prayer word for word.

It had been part of Alex's final request that he was buried as a Ranger with all their rights and customs.

"May the gods watch over them and lead them on the path beyond," she continued.

It was now time for any final words. Cameron glanced up at Ferrell who decided to exercise his right to go first. He walked forward and knelt beside the headstone.

"I know what you would say, don't get emotional on me now, James. No matter what went down you kept me level. Your council, experience and friendship will be deeply missed. Peace be with you, old friend," Ferrell said quietly.

After finishing he rose to his feet and retook his place next to Cameron. It was now her turn. The Telekinetic walked forward trying to dry her tear stained eyes. Like Ferrell she knelt next to her mentors final resting place.

"I am so sorry, I know the sniper round was meant for me," Cameron whispered and tried not to break down.

"How am I going to do this without you?" she asked, but no response could be heard. Cameron tried to continue but broke down into tears at the thought of never seeing him again.

"You were a brother, my mentor and my friend," Cameron sniffled, "I love you and always will."

She wiped her eyes and took to her feet. Cameron took a moment to regain her composure and rejoined Ferrell.

With the ceremony concluded, Ferrell and Cameron turned. They made their way back inside the compound. They walked silently through the hallways and up half a dozen flights of stairs and stopped at the entrance to Alex's room.

Ferrell pulled out a key from his pocket and unlocked the door. He turned the handle and pushed the door open. Cameron could smell the lingering scent of Alex's cologne waft through the open door. A multiplicity of memories and feelings rushed back to Cameron in that moment.

Ferrell stepped past her and entered Alex's room. She followed the Slave Lord in, shut the door, and stood motionless awaiting his instructions.

"Come here Cameron," Ferrell said and motioned for her to join him.

He reached down, pulled a bottle of whisky off the nightstand and made his way to a small bar. Cameron walked over to the bed, sat down and gazed across at Ferrell. She was surprised to see Ferrell pour two drinks, he turned back and offered her a glass.

Cameron cautiously accepted the beverage and held it.

"To Alex Sheridan," Ferrell said and raised his glass.

"May he never be forgotten," Cameron finished.

She took a deep breath and tried not to cough as the alcoholic beverage burned her throat.

"Did you know Alex was buzzed eighty percent of the time?" Ferrell asked with a chuckle, "I started to wonder over the years if he could do the job sober."

He turned back to the bar and made himself another drink.

"I suspected," Cameron replied.

She was intrigued by Ferrell's friendly, bordering on kind mannerisms. Alex and Cameron had always been close, sometimes inseparable, but

Ferrell had kept the position of master and slave ever present. He took another large gulp and stared down at her, clearly deep in thought.

"We have a very interesting conversation ahead of us Cameron Lynn Summers," Ferrell stated.

The Ranger's heart fluttered at the sound of her full name being used.

"In this conversation I am considering you an equal, you can talk to me just as Alex would. I need his honesty and his council, but he was taken from us," Ferrell explained.

As much as the option to speak her mind greatly interested Cameron, she decided to remain silent.

Ferrell noticed and downed his drink. He turned back to make another before continuing.

"On Daigys you passed every physical and mental test we could think of. Down to making you wade in swamp water. Alex's idea," Ferrell said with a laugh.

Dick, Cameron thought to herself, *I hate mud.*

She took a sip of her drink, still disgusted by the thought.

"The next part is from me, and the question I need answered. Can you, in time fill in the shoes of Alex? Can you move past being a slave and become my enforcer?" he questioned.

Cameron was overall surprised at his statement.

"So, what do you want from me?" she replied in a firm, yet cautious tone.

Ferrell took another large sip of his drink before he responded.

"I need to be able to trust you. I need to know you will not betray me. I need honesty, Cameron."

Something snapped in her mind at his statement. *Years of being suppressed, pushed around, told to be silent, and now you want my honesty?* Cameron screamed in her mind. The fire inside her continued to burn until it had to be let out.

"You want damned honesty? Then let's cut the Draith shit Ferrell," Cameron snapped and took to her feet.

Ferrell held his ground and did not respond.

"I'm a slave. Owned and controlled by you. My only living family member has been locked alone on the fourth level of the lion's den since I've arrived. I haven't seen him in years, haven't even talked to him.

Honestly, I don't know if my Grandfather is even alive. Anymore I take that on childish faith," Cameron spouted back with fire in her voice.

Ferrell remained emotionless to her rant. He turned around and poured at least two shots into his glass. He took a breath and drank the sharp whisky.

Cameron looked down at her glass and realized it had barely been touched. She downed her drink and placed it on the bar for Ferrell to refill. Ferrell glanced down at the glass, to Cameron and back to the bar.

"Atta girl," Ferrell said in a dry tone.

He promptly filled the glass with ice and poured two shots into it. The ice cracked and popped as the alcohol trickled over it. Ferrell handed the glass back to Cameron. He picked up his drink and walked over to the bed. He sat on the edge and continually nursed the bitter whisky.

Cameron turned and observed Ferrell. He sat there with his forearms resting on his legs. He had a blank stare which was focused on the adjacent wall.

"You're right, Cameron. There is no point in lying to you. Yes, you are damn right I used Hayden to control you. Why? Because you are the most dangerous risk I have ever attempted," Ferrell replied, almost scared of the thought.

"You're afraid of me?" Cameron questioned.

Ferrell shook his head.

"Not of you, but of the overwhelming power you have. I've known from day one, you would either make me extraordinarily rich or be the death of me," he confessed.

Cameron smiled at the comment and took another drink.

"You are the most valuable possession I have. I know you hate being referred to as such, but that's the stone-cold truth," Ferrell said and downed the rest of his whisky.

Cameron took a larger gulp at his honesty.

"If worse comes to worse, I'm going to launch you at the enemy and get the hell out of the way," Ferrell said with a laugh.

Cameron could not help but smile at his buzzed, almost carefree reactions but she knew he was not joking and would do it without a second thought.

"And if I help you. If I took his place. What's in it for me?" she pressed and took full advantage of speaking openly.

"Freedom," he replied without hesitation.

Cameron was floored by his statement. *Freedom?* she thought with disbelief.

"After everything you just said, you would free me?" Cameron questioned skeptically.

"Yes, in ten fifteen years when Hayden dies. How am I going to control you then?" he asked.

"You can't," Cameron replied and followed his line of thought.

Both held their gaze eyes locked, each strategizing.

Ferrell's comm sounded and broke the silence between them. He reached back and pulled the device off his belt.

"Yes," Ferrell said abruptly into the comm.

"Incoming transmission form Garocus," Sargus responded.

"Inform Adrian I will be in the throne room shortly," Ferrell replied.

He turned off the device before Sargus could confirm. Still holding the comm, Ferrell turned his gaze back to Cameron.

"Do we have an understanding, Cameron?" Ferrell asked.

There was only one answer she could give him. The only one that made sense.

"We do," Cameron replied in a timely and respectful manner.

"Then grab your coat," Ferrell said.

He took to his feet, downed his drink and placed the empty glass neatly on the bar. He passed Cameron and opened the door.

"Let's go meet the self-proclaimed master of the universe," Ferrell said with added sarcasm.

Cameron picked up her coat. With one seamless motion she whipped it around and put it on with practiced swag.

With a few sped-up-steps, Cameron caught up with Ferrell in a couple of paces. They made their way through the hallways and into the throne room. They walked through the wooden set of doors, down the stairs and across to the hexagon platform. Ferrell jogged up the steps and took his seat on the wooden throne. Cameron quickly followed and stood to his right. She was a few levels below him and kept her hands clasped in front of her.

"Activate transmission," Ferrell commanded.

Seconds later, an image of Adrian appeared and filled the throne room. His blond hair was flat with only the front sticking up. He was wearing a skintight white shirt, with his arms crossed. Cameron could tell by his gaze Adrian was not in a good mood. He glared over at her then back to Ferrell.

"I know how much you like theatrics Ferrell, but please have your Ranger lose the disguise," Adrian said in a blunt tone and motioned at Cameron's hood.

She looked over at Ferrell who nodded his permission. Cameron took off her coat and tossed it to the far side of the hexagon. Cameron turned her eyes back to Adrian. He lusted over the Ranger from her white cap sleeve shirt to her abyss colored boots.

"As they use to say back on Old Earth, your jailbait, girl," Adrian said with a chuckle.

He gave one final glance at Cameron before he turned his attention back to the Slave Lord.

"So, James, how is your little conflict with Colin Trails going?" he asked and changed the subject.

His tone was direct, and it was clear this was the reason Adrian had called.

"Why do you ask? Does my little war concern you?" Ferrell replied condescendingly.

"Don't dick around, Ferrell. He's not just destroying our slave trade profits, but he's also attacked a half dozen Ninth Faction planets," Adrian's voice boomed.

"Where are the Narairians? They have a bigger fleet then most of Known-Space combined," Ferrell pressed, but Adrian shook his head in response.

"I'm not aggravating the insects just to fix your mistakes, James," Adrian retorted, "have you tried a diplomatic approach?"

"I have," Ferrell shot back.

"And what were his terms?" Adrian asked impatiently.

"He's demanding compensation for the slaves and Accaren guards he lost on Daigys, as well as the other planets we have attacked. Totaling it up, it comes to three hundred million Ingots," Ferrell replied.

Adrian looked down as he thought about the math.

"It would hurt, but it's doable. What else does he want?" the blond man asked.

"There lies the issue, Trails is also demanding the slave he tried to force himself on when this all got started," Ferrell replied.

"I don't see the issue, James?" Adrian asked with a blank stare.

"It's who he wants," Ferrell replied.

Cameron could tell Adrian was confused by Ferrell's statement. He put his hands on his hips. As if Cameron could see a lightbulb go off. Adrian turned to her then back to Ferrell.

"You've got to be shitting me. Does he know what race she is?" Adrian said in an angered tone.

"The good news is no," Ferrell replied.

Adrian merely laughed at his response.

"That is an overall optimistic view to say there is ANY good news. Except for the choice you need to make," Adrian retorted.

"I'm not giving her up," Ferrell replied in equal fashion.

Cameron's heart skipped a beat at Ferrell's response.

"I know you have a fascination with Rangers, Ferrell, but it's time to grow up," Adrian replied in a condescending manner.

"That's not going to happen," Ferrell said, to Cameron's shock and amazement.

She was not sure if it was the alcohol, or the grief of losing Alex, but Ferrell held his ground. Adrian crossed his arms as he contemplated the debate.

"You're going to say that with everything that you've screwed up over the past few years? Let's count together. First off you allowed Shelby Pierce to escape your custody," he retorted and kept track with his fingers, "and understand James, I have not reaped the harvest on that shit storm. Moving forward, your enforcer was murdered at a Ninth Faction resort, and do we need to recap what you've done to the Accaren border?"

"I will handle what has transpired," Ferrell proclaimed.

"I don't think you understand, James. There is a plan and the war of the Slave Lords is threatening her plan. I'm getting push back from higher up. She has given me a choice and now I'm in the same shit hole as you," Adrian said in a vague manner.

Ferrell leaned forward. Cameron could see the strategies forming in his mind and tried to find the most successful talk path.

"And what did the Demonic Princess say?" Ferrell replied in a calm tone.

"Let me simplify this for you. If you cannot fix this, I will. If I do, I swear to God I will rebuild the Ninth Faction from the ground up," Adrian threatened.

Cameron looked over at Ferrell who had a subtle grin.

"I don't believe you, Adrian. First off Alex Sheridan was killed by former Human military elite. Also, as for Shelby Peirce, what kind of sick, deplorable son of a bitch keeps one of his oldest friends imprisoned for over a decade. Finally, I will win this war in my own way and on my own terms. Best part, you're not going to try and stop me," Ferrell yelled back arrogantly.

"Why would you—" Adrian stopped mid-sentence.

He looked over at Cameron and shook his head.

"Little early to be playing that card, isn't it, James?" Adrian questioned.

"A Ranger-Telekinetic is the one force in Known-Space which has the power to beat the living shit out of your arrogant ass," Ferrell retorted.

Cameron's heart leapt into her throat at Ferrell's counter.

Oh shit, the young Ranger thought to herself, but she kept her pose. Blank stare with her eyes fixed on the super powered Human.

Adrian held equal calm. He took a few steps back, lowered his head, and whispered in Latin. Adrian's eyes lit up with a violent red and matched the light of his surroundings. Within seconds, lightning surrounded him, and a red tornado filled the room. The cyclone rose transporting Adrian off Garocus.

Cameron knew what she had to do. It did not matter if the odds were a hundred to one against her. Alex had warned her about Adrian years ago. The Crimson Syndicate were basically demigods. Each one over a thousand years old, with the knowledge and experience to match. Not to mention they were experts in almost every martial-art and had a dimensional shield.

Cameron glanced back at Ferrell who also had a hint of uncertainty in his eyes. Her gaze whipped back to the room, but she saw nothing.

"Don't worry. He'll be here any second," Ferrell said and followed her gaze.

As Ferrell predicted a red cyclone touched down in the center of the throne room. It spun around while arcs branched off and struck the marble floor. After a few seconds, the cyclone vanished and left Adrian standing in the center of the room. His eyes matched the cyclone, before turning back to their brown coloring. Cameron raised her hands in defense, but Adrian remained motionless with his hands behind his back.

"I'm calling your bluff, James, and by doing so will teach you a lesson in respect," Adrian said in a stone-cold voice.

"I will never let that happen," Cameron interjected fiercely and brazenly took a few steps down the stairs.

She stood in front of Ferrell, raised her fists in defense and put as much intimidation as she could into her statement. To her surprise, Cameron's words silenced Adrian.

"You told me it took you and two other members of the Syndicate to take down Simon Cail. Let me handle this my way. I'll deal with Trails, we don't have to do this," Ferrell postured.

"You opened this door Ferrell, and by God we will pass through it."

Adrian aimed his right arm at Cameron and fired a red energy sphere. The Ranger dove forward and rolled down the stairs. She hit the bottom with a thud and made a quick recovery. She activated her ascension and took hold of the blond man. She used all her strength and hurled Adrian to the left, but his weight caught her off guard. It felt like she tried to throw a slave barge, if not two or three.

Adrian stumbled to the side unfazed by the assault. Before Cameron knew it, two additional spheres flew toward her rapidly.

Unable to dodge, Cameron was hit on the left shoulder as well as her right hip. She yelped out in pain as the energy lifted her off the ground and launched her back into the hexagon platform.

A sharp crack sounded as two of Cameron's ribs broke on impact. Cameron looked for her target who rapidly approached. She raised her arm, but Adrian grabbed on and twisted it painfully to the side. He reached down with his other hand, gripped her neck tightly and lifted her thin frame off the floor.

Cameron gasped for air as her feet dangled. She tried to break his hold, but instead his grip tightened.

"I was truly scared, Ferrell. To think you just risked your entire empire on this child makes me sick," Adrian said with a laugh.

His grip continued to tighten. Cameron's eyes stayed locked on his, void of desperation or any cry for mercy. His eyes met with hers, and in that gaze her defiance was clear.

"Damned Rangers. If I had my way, I would wipe out the whole of your conceded, self-absorbed race from the galaxy itself," Adrian cursed.

Deep inside of her a fire grew. With power and strength, Cameron gasped and let out a high pitch scream. From her body erupted a massive shockwave. Cameron had reached her second ascension as a Ranger-Telekinetic. The wave pushed Adrian back, and forced him to release Cameron. She fell to the ground and with one motion threw her arms forward.

A wave of telekinetic energy crashed into Adrian. The force of the hit lifted him off the ground and threw him in the direction of the main door. Cameron quickly regained her footing and started forward. Before he could recover, Cameron picked up one of Ferrell's life sized, solid rock statues and hurled it at the Syndicate member.

While it was in motion, Cameron did the same with the next one in line. The marble figures swung around and crashed into his shield with the force of a dozen energy missiles. While he was blinded, Cameron grabbed the third statue. She spun around and repeated the process. On the third spin she let go and threw the figure with even greater force. It slammed into Adrian, lifted him off the ground and launched him through the main doors. A loud crash sounded as the solid wood shattered into hundreds of pieces.

Cameron continued forward and knew she could not let him recover. She heard debris move and soon after Adrian stumbled back to the doorway. He gave a mild shake of his head and to amazement wiped blood off his lip. He looked down at his stained finger and back to Cameron.

With anger, Adrian said a different phrase in Latin. His eyes lit up with brilliant red and dimensional energy filled his body.

Adrian charged forward at top speed. Cameron tried to throw him, but each time he only moved a meter either way. It was not long before Adrian was in striking distance. He opened with a right hook, but Cameron dodged the attack and threw a telekinetic-punch. The energy hit the center of his shield and pushed him back a meter.

He lunged forward but just as before Cameron shifted her body just in the nick of time and dodged the powerful hit. While she recovered, Adrian shifted his body and kicked her in the chest.

The hit lifted Cameron off the ground and threw her back a half dozen meters. Cameron coughed and was in extreme pain. She gripped her broken chest and had trouble moving.

Adrian made his way forward, gripped her white shirt and lifted her off the ground. As she rose Adrian cocked back his arm and landed a massive blow.

Cameron's head whipped to the side and her body went limp. She felt blood drip from her mouth as she barely held onto consciousness.

He let go, and the battered Ranger fell to the cold hard floor. She forced herself to her hands and knees as she stared down at the blood-stained tile. All of it her own. Adrian kicked her in the ribs and launched her like a ball across the throne room. Cameron rolled onto her back and cried out in agony, but no one could help her.

Adrian walked forward, grabbed Cameron by the shirt and drug her to the base of the hexagon platform.

"Here is your pet Ranger," Adrian sneered, but Ferrell remained silent.

Adrian knelt on top of her and cocked back his arm.

"Any final words?" he questioned.

"Screw off stupid Human," she muttered with a blood-filled smile.

Adrian lost control of his emotions and threw a knockout blow into Cameron's jaw. Everything went blank and the teen Ranger was rendered unconscious.

* * *

Cameron's eyes flashed open. She took a pain filled breath, but instantly coughed. She could tell by the bright overhead lights that she was in one of the medical bays of the fortress.

Two rhino-bred Tuskerons stood over her. She tried to move but was too badly injured.

A Human doctor walked over, examined her wounds and revealed a small grey injector. Cameron's body tensed up as she saw it.

"Hold her down," the doctor commanded.

The Tuskerons firmly put their three fingered hands on her and pressed Cameron against the table. He was holding a vile of medical-nanites, or better known as the `last resort'. The doctor pressed the nanite injector on Cameron's chest and pulled the trigger. Cameron let out a high pitch scream as the nanites forcibly moved her ribs back into place. The doctor pulled out a second injector and moved to her shoulder.

Cameron shook her head as a plea for him to stop his pending action. The doctor ignored her and gave her a second dose of nanites. Cameron could not suppress the pain any further. She screamed at the top of her lungs. As she lay there unable to imagine a worse fate, her vision blurred once again.

I'm not going to pass out. I'm not going to pass out, Cameron repeated to herself, but it was no use and within a few seconds Cameron lost consciousness.

* * *

Cameron's eye's opened slowly. At first sight she was not sure where she was. After her eyes had time to focus, Cameron realized she was in her room. Everything in her head was jumbled. She sat up, moved to the edge of the bed and lifted her shirt. Cameron inspected her ribs. There was still minor bruising, but the nanites seemed to have fully healed her. As she looked over the wound, the memories from her fight with Adrian came rushing back in series of images.

"Oh gods," Cameron said out loud and was surprised she still walked amongst the living.

She stood up and limped over to the mirror. Her face had partially healed, while the left side of her jaw was badly bruised. Her right eye struggled to stay open. Upon closer inspection, Cameron could see the faded indent of Adrian's knuckles.

Unsure of what day it was, Cameron made her way to the data-pad and activated it. It had been fifty hours since the encounter.

"Better check in with Ferrell," Cameron said to herself.

She quickly straightened up her hair and opened the door. Cameron stopped dead in her tracks at the sight of seven rhino-bred Tuskerons standing guard. Cameron looked for something recognizable, and after a few seconds saw Sargus who lumbered toward her.

"What's going on?" Cameron asked with concern.

"We were instructed to escort you to Ferrell," Sargus replied and held a pair of restraints, "I was ordered to bind your hands."

Cameron was reluctant to go cuffed and crossed her arms.

"On who's order?" Cameron questioned.

"James Ferrell," Sargus replied.

The other guards stepped forward and gripped their weapons tighter.

Something is wrong, Cameron's mind panicked, a*m I ready to make my stand here?*

Cameron was ninety percent sure she could deal with the Tuskerons.

But then what? she asked herself.

Cameron decided to give in. She turned around and placed her hands behind her back.

"You mean on behalf of Adrian Quin's orders," Cameron said in a snotty, almost annoyed tone.

Sargus grunted something in his own native language and secured the Telekinetic. Cameron was escorted through the halls of the compound until she reached the throne room. The newly repaired double doors opened and swung inward. They walked down the small set of stairs and up to the hexagon platform.

Ferrell sat on his throne with Adrian directly to his right.

"Hello Cameron," Ferrell said in an emotionless tone.

"Have I done something wrong?" Cameron asked with concern, but Ferrell remained silent.

"Ferrell," Cameron pressed and tried to gain some form of reaction.

"It wasn't you necessarily, but that doesn't mean you're not affected by his actions," Adrian interjected cryptically.

Cameron was not sure of what he meant and looked back at Ferrell with confusion.

"Effective immediately. I am selling you to Colin Trails," Ferrell said bluntly.

Cameron did not have any words. She did not have any thoughts and merely stood. Jaw dropped.

"What?!" Cameron stammered, "how could you do this to me?"

Her entire world was caving in and she felt there was nothing she could do to stop it.

"For the past two days I've been in heated negotiations with that arrogant douche bag," Ferrell ranted and got lost in his own anger, "after hours of arguing we came to terms. Apart from a lot of money, the one thing Trails would not let go was his infatuation with you."

Cameron felt physically sick by the end of his statement. Infatuation was too kind a word for what Trails wanted to do to her. What he wanted to take from her.

He's a sick, twisted Human who allows himself to be controlled by his own base needs. Considering what he did to Nora. She was beaten to a pulp, raped, and left for dead in a storage room. Cameron thought with unimaginable hatred and fear.

"I won't—"

Ferrell raised his hand and silenced her. Simultaneously the Tuskerons raised their assault-rifles and aimed them at her. Seven barrels pointed at her head and chest.

"You will listen, or I will have the Tuskerons take turns beating you in to submission!" Ferrell's voice boomed.

Cameron grit her teeth and remained silent as she tried to control her anger, but there were still questions she needed answered. First, was Colin still under the false impression that she was Human? Or did Ferrell tell him the truth, robbing Cameron of her only advantage. The second was more important.

What about my Grandfather*?* Cameron's mind panicked.

Cameron knew Ferrell would allow one more statement, but she had to phrase it perfectly.

"Sargus will escort you to Trails' ship on landing pad ten," Ferrell commanded.

He motioned for the guards to escort Cameron out. Sargus grabbed her by the arm and pulled her to the side. Cameron held her ground, rolled her shoulder and broke free of Sargus's grip.

"So, everything you said in Alex's room was a lie?" Cameron yelled and gave up on the phrasing, "the promises that were made, the understanding we came to?"

"You forget, Cameron. I don't have to hold to anything I say. I own you," Ferrell hissed.

Sargus took a firmer grip and forcefully pulled her back in the direction of the door.

"What about my Grandfather?" Cameron yelled back with fury.

The Slave Lord did not answer and kept silent.

"Ferrell!" Cameron screamed as she reached the door.

"I had no more use for him," Ferrell replied before Sargus and the other Tuskerons removed her from the throne room.

Cameron's heart sank, and her eyes swelled with tears at his response.

Stupid b*astard,* Cameron thought with hatred. She was confused and felt betrayed by Ferrell's actions. *But who said Ferrell made that choice?*

Adrian was the true evil and she knew it.

They continued toward landing pad ten while Sargus kept a firm grip on Cameron's arm.

"I can walk on my own, Sargus." Cameron snapped in a cold, bitter tone.

One that was consumed with pain and overwhelming hatred.

Sargus raised his arm and stopped the rest of the guards. He let go of her arm and looked down with his jet-black eyes.

"Sorry," Sargus muttered.

"It's not your fault. Adrian's just a dick," Cameron said in frustration.

She got a chuckle from Sargus and the other Tuskeron guards.

"Let's do this," Cameron said and peered over at the powerlift.

Cameron knew there was no point in fighting, not yet. She needed to save her strength for the battle to come.

I will die before I let that man touch me, her mind blazed with fury, g*ods, if I make it out of this, I'll make Ferrell pay for what he's done.*

The group walked into the powerlift and took the short ride to the landing pad. The doors opened, and they walked out onto the metal platform. The weather matched her emotions. Heavy wind, with what appeared to be a sandstorm on the horizon.

In the center of the platform was a small Accaren transport. The side hatch was open, and three Accarens stood at the base of the ramp. Each one outfitted with their native blue armor. The lead Accaren stepped forward, followed closely by his men. They stopped where the pad met with the bridge. Cameron recognized him as Colin's bodyguard, Damarious Ta'ag. He was taller than the others, with tribal leadership markings on his shoulders.

"It's about time, brute," Damarious's voice sounded through the speaker built into his helmet.

It sounded cold and mechanical.

Sargus motioned for his guards to stop. They followed his command, and each kept a firm grip on their weapon. Sargus took hold of Cameron's arm and drug her forward. They continued along the metal bridge. Sargus pushed Cameron forward into the cold armored hands of Damarious.

The lead Accaren passed Cameron off to the second guard and stared at the Tuskeron. The other guards forcefully moved Cameron in the direction of the shuttle.

"You have the Human. Now leave," Sargus's voice rumbled.

"You're little more than a herbivore. You don't scare me Tuskeron," he retorted with a laugh.

As Cameron and the guards approached the ramp, the Accaren to her right reached down and put his hand on the back of her leg. He slowly moved his hand up and cupped her butt.

Cameron put her right leg forward and tripped the guard. The armored Accaren fell forward onto the ramp and rolled to the side.

"Uk'!" Cameron screamed down at him and used Accaren profanity.

As the word left her lips, she felt the second Accaren's grip. His hand tightened around her neck and lifted her off the ground. The first Accaren stood back up and stepped forward aggressively toward her.

"Stop! Trails wants the Human in one piece," Damarious yelled back.

A sigh of relief filled Cameron's mind. Not only did Damarious use the term `Human' but Trails wanted her unharmed. Cameron could tell by their body-language neither of the guards were happy with the Tribal leader's command but followed it all the same.

The second Accaren released his grip on the Telekinetic and both guards' drug her up the ramp. She entered the shuttle and saw two shielded cells at the rear of the vessel. Overall the ship was small with a half dozen seats. One of the guards broke away and sat in the pilot's chair. He flipped three switches and prepped the ship for launch.

The second guard kept a firm grip on Cameron and escorted her back to the left cell. The guard took hold of her cuffs and pressed his forearm against the back of her neck. Cameron stumbled forward into the wall of the ship. The Accaren held his grip and pinned her firmly.

The guard let go of the cuffs and used that hand to search her for weapons.

"I can't believe we waited three hours for this scrawny Human bitch," the pilot complained in Accaren.

Cameron kept silent and did not reveal her understanding of their native language.

Cameron clenched her jaw in fury as the guard slowed his search around specific areas of her body.

"Look at the bright side. Maybe Trails will let us take turns after he's through," the guard said in a dark tone.

"Don't count on it," Damarious retorted in basic upon entering the ship.

He immediately closed the hatch and took off his helmet. Damarious had a rough, scarred face with blue octagons under his eyes. Cameron could tell by the way he moved and by his voice that Damarious was hard as stone. Not one hint of emotion as if it had been cleansed by fire.

"It amazes me the amount of time Trails has obsessed about this one parafek. She's not worth a half percent of the credits wasted on this conflict. When Trails gets done with her, she won't be worth anything," Damarious said with disgust.

"Too bad," the guard muttered.

He ran his hand down her leg to her boots.

Cameron wanted to fight. She wanted to swear and tell him to stop. In the end, she knew it was futile and would only aggravate the Accaren and make matters worse.

After what felt like an eternity, the guard finished his search for weapons and equipment. He took hold of her restraints and led her into the cell.

"Cuffs on or off?" the guard clarified.

Damarious looked over at her and pondered the question.

Please say off. Cameron prayed with overwhelming hatred. It was a better scenario to fight three Accarens in a shuttle, versus unknown numbers where they were going.

"I'm going to let Trails do that. One would think she's his damned birthday present. His childish excitement in forcing Ferrell to agree to his terms makes me sick," Damarious said in an overly annoyed tone.

Damn it, Cameron swore in her mind at the unfavorable answer.

The guard pushed Cameron in and activated the cell. He left and joined his comrade at the helm. The shuttle lifted off and set course for Senia. The headquarters of Colin Trails. The vessel shook as the pilot made the jump to subspace. The motion caused Cameron to stumble in her cell, but she was able to maintain her balance.

Damarious caught sight of the movement and glanced over at her. Their eyes locked, and Cameron could tell something was not sitting well with him. She did not know if it was his overall mood or if it was the look of defiance she maintained. Damarious peered at her in the same way Conrad's Accaren slaves had.

It had never been proven that Accarens could sense Rangers, but in her experience, they guessed right more often the not.

He took to his feet and walked over to the cell door. He stood as tall as Alex with a matching build. The Accaren aggressively crossed his arms as their eyes stayed locked. Cameron tilted her head to the side as the expression of defiance remained.

"How did you serve James Ferrell?" Damarious questioned.

"I served him in a variety of ways," Cameron replied.

"Such as?" he pressed.

"I was his personal slave. The sick things he made me do," Cameron responded and generalized the truth.

She could see a cold understanding in Damarious's eyes.

Ferrell may have made her work as an enforcer, but he never abused his slaves sexually. This was a lie she needed Damarious to believe. If he found out the truth, she knew her hands would never be freed and in turn she would not be able to use her abilities. If they knew how much information she had on Ferrell, Cameron would be tortured, raped and beaten to death with clubs.

It was the Accaren's favorite form of execution for her race and gender.

"Right before the raid on Araka, I remember a cloaked figure back around the holo-pad on Camus. Your build is nearly identical. She was next to Alex Sheridan, which tells me she was a Ranger," Damarious said heading down the talk path Cameron hoped he wouldn't.

"Do you really think Ferrell would be stupid enough to give up a Ranger to his mortal enemy?" Cameron retorted and belittled his question.

"What happened to her?" he interrogated.

"She was killed on Oc'tal'ia. The same time as Alex Sheridan," Cameron lied.

"How can I trust you?" he questioned further.

"I'm sentenced to be beaten and raped by a sick perverted man. Why would I waste my last few hours of life answering your stupid questions! If I were a Ranger, I would wipe the floor with all three of you!" Cameron screamed back.

Damarious remained emotionless and gauged her reactions.

After a moment, Damarious and the other Accarens laughed at her threat.

"Sure, you would," he sneered.

The Accaren left her and returned to his seat. Cameron glared at him for a moment before she turned her mind back to finding a way to escape.

* * *

The vessel burst out of subspace in orbit of Senia. From her cell, Cameron could see three Accaren cruisers through the front viewport. The shuttle flew passed the patrols and down to the planet.

Cameron had never been to Senia, but from what she had read, the planet had grass lands in the northern hemisphere, with impassible mountains to the south. The rest of the planet was covered in deep unexplored oceans.

Shit. We're heading to the south, Cameron thought.

It was the icing on the cake. Cameron hated the cold and was dressed for Camus. She kept a line of sight fixed on the viewport and desperately searched for a glimpse of their destination.

They flew over thousands of kilometers of snow-covered peaks until they finally came to their target. Cameron's eyes fell upon a four-level structure built into the side of the mountain. The mansion was of wood and stone. Other than the shuttle there were no other forms of access and made escape suicide.

The shuttle swooped down and landed gently on the small two vessel pad. Damarious walked to her cell and lowered the shield. He grabbed her arm and drug her out toward the door. He walked her down the ramp and passed her off to an awaiting Accaren.

It was freezing. Continuous snow filled the gusts, melting on to her skin and hair. Cameron looked over at Damarious who was busy talking with one of his men.

After looking around the structure, Cameron estimated Trails had no more than twenty Accaren stationed at the base.

It's a long shot, but I could take on twenty Accarens in waves, Cameron thought with daring optimism. Her bigger concern was the three cruisers in orbit.

Her clothes were soaked. As the seconds ticked by Cameron started going numb. Damarious turned and noticed her shaking.

"Looks like you're already wet aren't you, parafek?" he sneered vulgarly.

A volcano of disgust, nausea and deplorability all encompassed within a sphere of rage erupted inside her at the crude remark. To make matters worse, he got a laugh from the guards around him.

Cameron could not control her anger anymore and spouted off a slew of Accaren profanity. She spoke of his mother and sister, and the intimate relations they shared with aliens. She cursed his profession, title, race, and creed. Damarious was taken aback and was clearly insulted not only by her choice of profanity but that she did so fluently in their own language.

"Human pride, bitch!" Cameron screamed and quoted her genetic cousins' favorite phrase.

Damarious stepped forward and backhanded the Ranger. Cameron's head whipped to the side. She cried out in pain at being struck by his armored fist.

"Take her back to the dark room," Damarious commanded.

Fear and anxiety filled her mind as the guard pulled her across the landing pad and down the hallways of the fortress. Unlike Camus, the base was built for Accaren living. The ceilings were only two and a half meters in height. The walls were made of wood with Draith size chunks of rock taking place of the wood in some sections.

Cameron's eyes scanned and memorized the winding passages. Her heart raced as they neared their destination. She wanted to run, to scream, but she knew her best chance at survival was to get Colin one on one. As much as that terrified her, she knew it was the only way.

They stopped at a set of wooden doors. Cameron's heart pounded as the guard unlocked the room. The door swung inward, and the guard pushed her in. Cameron stumbled and somehow kept her footing. She found herself in a rectangular room built into the mountain. The room was simply made with a bed, sink, and a bear skin rug in the middle of the room.

Cameron fought the urge to puke as she saw the multiplicity of stains on the rug. The lighting was dim. At the back of the room Cameron saw the tall shadow of Colin Trails. His thick beard blended in with the darkness. His menacing eyes were locked on her as a Draith would eye its prey.

"We meet again, Cameron. Our last encounter was interrupted. I promise you that won't happen again," Colin said in a cold, gruff voice, "Alex Sheridan is not here to save you."

It sent a chill down Cameron's spine.

Colin stepped into the light of the fire and stood on the other side of the rug.

"Come here," he said and motioned with his hand.

She was at the point of tears and could not move.

"Cameron, come here!" Colin yelled in a deep threatening tone.

She had to. She could not show weakness. Colin walked forward and stood in front of his spoils of war. Colin was tall for a Human and weighed three times what Cameron did.

He put his cold, rough hands on her waist, up her sides and to her shoulders. His hand moved to the left strap of her tank top. He gripped on tight and prepared to rip it.

"No!" Cameron yelled back and tried to pull away.

It was no use. The material strap broke like a twig under pressure. Colin proceeded to put his hand down her shirt.

"No!" Cameron screamed louder.

But Colin was not compelled to stop and slid his other hand down her pants.

"Stupid Human coward!" she screamed at the top of her lungs.

Colin paused his exploration and removed his hands. He stood in silence and stared down at Cameron's impudence.

"What did you say?" he sneered.

"You're afraid of me. Some hundred and twenty-pound girl," Cameron mocked.

Offended by the insult, Colin stood at full height and was prepared to strike her.

"Why else would you tie my hands? Your scared I'll beat you to a bloody pulp!" she taunted more and more aggressively.

"Do you really want me to beat you before I take you?" Colin growled.

"I'll pound your ass into the ground and spit into your blood-stained skull!" Cameron yelled with fury.

"Fine!" Colin yelled back without a moment's thought. He spun her around in anger and took off the cuffs. He whipped her back around. Before Cameron could react, he threw a punch that struck her across the face.

Her head whipped to the side and Cameron found herself on the ground. Blood dripping from the side of her mouth.

"Is this what you wanted? Did Ferrell like it rough too?" he mocked.

Cameron looked back to her captor with a cracked lip and devious blood-filled smile.

"What are you—" Colin was cut off as Cameron lifted him off the ground.

Cameron took to her feet and used her ascension to hold him in place.

"You're a—"

"Damn right, dick. Now I'm going to kill every one of you sick, twisted child loving bastards!" Cameron screamed in response and cut him off once again.

The room shook as her anger grew. Fear crossed over Colin's face in waves as he realized his mistake.

Colin turned white as a ghost as Cameron lifted him higher.

"I've seen men like you my entire life! I've bowed, scraped, and forced to serve. Desperately praying every night I'd never be alone with a villain like you!" she yelled with fury.

Cameron paced back and forth and held her prey tightly.

"I've always had the power to stop you, I was never allowed to use It. That time is past," the Ranger sneered.

"You don't want to do this," Colin postured.

"I've got nothing else to lose," Cameron said honestly.

She had said her peace, it was now time for action. With a sharp motion of her forearm. Cameron launched Colin at full speed toward the door. The three hundred plus pound man crashed through the doorway with the force of a Tuskeron. The sound of bones cracking could be heard as Trails slammed into the solid oak. Upon impact the door broke into half a dozen pieces.

He rolled into the hallway and came to a stop at the adjacent wall. Colin cried out on impact. He sat up slowly and was clearly in agony.

Cameron could tell by his joint placement the throw had dislocated his shoulder and broke his hip. Cameron walked forward and used her ascension to effortlessly lift him off the ground. Colin whimpered in pain and tried to grip his shoulder.

What was his pain to her? Absolutely nothing.

"Cameron—"

The Telekinetic slammed him into the wall and silenced him.

"I can get you off this world—" he started.

Before Colin could finish, Cameron slammed him into the floor. She raised him back up, blood pouring from his mouth and nose.

"I'm done trusting men like you," Cameron sneered in a menacing tone.

Cameron knew she most likely would not survive the upcoming battle and refused to bow while she was still alive. Colin tried to speak but Cameron was done with their pointless conversation. She waved her hand to the left and hurled Colin at maximum velocity down the hallway. Cameron was able to take two full steps before she heard the blood curdling sound of Colin's bones break against the stone.

She walked forward and inspected his body. He had died on impact and his eyes were still open with blood running from his ears, nose and mouth.

"Told you," Cameron said and spit down on his corpse.

Cameron made her way back to the broken door. She stood over the wreckage for a moment before she found her perfect weapons. A solid wooden battering ram, two meters in length and weighed over a hundred pounds. The second piece of wood was rectangular and made a sufficient shield. Cameron used her abilities to pick up the weapons and started down the hallway, in the direction of the landing pad.

Cameron continued and turned left. Dead ahead she saw a lone Accaren Knight guarding the hallway. The Accaren raised his shield and fired a burst of orange energy. Cameron brought her wooden shield to bear and tanked the powerful hit. With her other hand, Cameron swung the wooden beam like a bat and struck the Accaren with the force of a dozen Tuskerons. The wooden battering ram hit the Knight in the chest and threw him back into the stone. Before he could recover, Cameron swung with the bat again and hit the Accaren square in the helmet. A loud ping sounded and the Accaren slumped to the floor. Upon closer inspection, Cameron saw a large dent in the Accaren's helm and knew it was the cause of death.

Hearing commotion, she whipped around to see four Accarens sprint around the corner. Cameron repeated her prior attack and swung the beam with full force to the left. It crushed into two of the Accarens and launched them back down the passage where they originated from. The two remaining guards braced themselves for attack, but Cameron was still faster. She swung the beam to the right and threw the Accarens into the cold unforgiving stone wall.

Two orange bursts came into view from the same hallway and shattered her custom bat. Cameron stepped forward in blind rage, she cocked back her shield and rounded the corner. Two more Accarens charged forward. Cameron shield bashed the first and launched him to the side. She turned to the second and threw her homemade shield at the Knight with a telekinetic punch. It hit the right side of his helmet and broke his neck instantly.

Cameron stood fists clenched. All she wanted to do was kill and make them pay for the injustice she had endured. Cameron turned and glared down the hallway at the sound of more Accarens. She sprinted forward and cared little for the incoming danger.

The first Accaren rounded the corner. The alien braced himself and fired a burst from his shield. Cameron dropped and slid on her knees and dodged the attack. Cameron could feel the heat of the powerful weapon as it came with in centimeters of her face.

She slid forward and used her abilities to lift the attacking Accaren. With one motion she swung her arm as if he were a Tuskeron's guards club and hurled the Accaren down the hallway. Cameron could hear sweet screams of chaos as the Accaren collided with six other guards.

In eloquent fury she moved through the Accarens. Screams from her victims echoed through the fortress as she used her ascension to crush, break, and destroy whatever was in her path. Whatever her rage could grip onto.

After what felt like a lifetime, she reached the door to the landing pad. Cameron reached forward and put her hand on the metal. Cameron could feel the presence of an Accaren behind her.

Cameron whipped around hands raised in defense. Her eyes opened wide as she saw Damarious a few meters away with his shield extended.

He fired a burst which impacted Cameron's chest. It pounded against her thin frame and threw her on to the cold landing pad.

"Parafek, was this your mission the entire time?" Damarious cursed upon and exited the building.

"Screw you. If you think I came here by choice you're nothing more than a stupid Human!" Cameron screamed back and was deeply insulted by his statement.

Damarious stood equally grieved and did not like being referred to as the lesser of the Humanoid races.

She scrambled to her feet but was hit with another shield blast. Cameron rolled further back, exhausted, bruised and broken. She gazed up at the black sky only to see endless waves of snow.

"Clearly my guards are inferior and can't deal with a Ranger of your ascension and class. I stand far beyond their pitiful station," Damarious's voice boomed, "I am Damarious Ta'ag, leader of the Ta'ag tribe and I will be damned if I'll let a Ranger defeat me."

"Then you'll be damned," Cameron screamed back.

Cameron scrapped to her feet but Damarious clipped her with the edge of his shield and threw her back to the hard metal pad. The Accaren stepped forward and lifted Cameron by the throat. She coughed and gasped for air.

"In the end, despite your race and your ability. I will bash your skull in like the common slave you are."

Cameron used what felt like her last breath and spit on his helmet. Damarious lost control. He elbowed her across the cheek and threw a heavy punch into her previously broken ribs. Cameron's body tensed up as she heard her ribs break further. She let out a high pitch scream and activated her second ascension. A constant energy wave erupted from her body. Damarious was caught off guard and was thrown back.

He rolled over six meters back toward the fortress. Cameron fell to her knees and gasped in endless pain. Her gaze lifted. She saw the Accaren struggle to his knees. She forced herself to her feet and used what little strength she had left to lift him off the ground. She lifted him over five meters in height. As if she were smashing a boulder, Cameron threw her arm downward and hurled Damarious onto the deck of the landing pad. She repeated the process six times. Each one harder than the next.

Cameron limped forward, clutched her ribs, and held Damarious stationary.

His helmet was broken, while his face was bleeding and mangled.

"There will be a reckoning for your actions this day," he said and coughed up blood, "the wrath of the Accarens is upon you, stupid Ranger."

"No one cares?" Cameron yelled back.

In that moment she focused her rage, pain and fear into her ability. With one motion of her hand, she launched Damarious off the edge of the platform. She could hear a murmured scream as he fell to his death. The sound gave her a feeling of joy and she let out a sigh of relief.

Tears rolled down her cheeks. Cameron screamed out in painstaking agony at the horrific events of the day. She turned back and searched desperately for an escape. Every ship was gone, with no other way off the freezing hell she was trapped on.

Her eyes turned to the skies above and she saw the lights of a vessel approach.

Oh gods, Cameron panicked.

After everything that had happened, she knew she did not have the strength for another conflict. The vessel swooped down with grace and hovered two dozen meters above the landing pad. The bottom of the ship opened, and six rhino-bred Tuskerons rappelled down. They landed and took up defensive positions. Cameron raised her hands but did not attack. A seventh individual rappelled and stood next to the behemoths.

Cameron grit her teeth in hatred as she recognized the black hair of her former master, James Ferrell.

"Stand down, Cameron. Your mission is over," Ferrell commanded.

Cameron stood in furious shock at the sight of the Slave Lord. His words ignited a fire inside her mind. She brazenly stepped forward and lifted him off the ground with her ascension.

"My mission?" Cameron screamed back.

The Tuskerons raised their assault-rifles but halted their fire with the motion of Ferrell's hand.

"You killed my Grandfather and traded me to a sick depraved bastard, and you expect me to obey you?" Cameron questioned.

"Hayden is alive," Ferrell stated.

Shocked by his words, Cameron released her grip and allowed Ferrell to continue.

"I never harmed your Grandfather," Ferrell confessed.

"But why—"

"Do you remember what I told you in Alex's room? If I must, I would throw you at the enemy and get the hell out of the way. Clearly, I was correct to do so," Ferrell retorted and peered over the carnage.

The Ranger remained silent and refused to yield.

"So, it will take proof, will it?" Ferrell replied.

He gave a motion of his hand and an eighth individual rappelled from the dropship. Cameron could not believe her eyes as they fell on her Grandfather. He had age significantly from the time she had seen him, but it was Hayden none the less. The Tuskerons kept him directly behind Ferrell and did not allow him to move forward.

"You've passed your final test with flying colors. You have ended the war with Colin Trails and have brought the Ninth Faction back to full strength.

The teen Ranger did not know what to think and shifted her vision between Ferrell and Hayden.

"Now bow and serve as my enforcer. Take hold of the role Alex and I always meant for you," Ferrell pressed.

Cameron's hands shook. Everything told her to throw him off the platform. To end it all including her own life.

"I hate you James Ferrell!" she screamed in response.

In that moment Cameron broke down. She fell to her knees and tears poured down her cheeks. Ferrell walked up and put his hand on her shoulder.

"Come Cameron," he said calmly, "we have a slave empire to rebuild." Cameron subtly nodded her head in submission.

Ferrell turned back and motioned for the guards to rappel up to the dropship. Cameron took to her feet and followed. She turned back and gave one final glance at Trail's fortress.

Ferrell noticed and matched her stance.

"What do you want to do with it?" Ferrell asked and referred to the building.

"Burn it," she replied void of all emotion, "burn it all to the ground."

Without a second thought, Cameron turned back and passed Ferrell. As she got closer her pace quickened and soon was in the arms of her Grandfather. He gave her a kiss on the forehead and looked over the mature Ranger she had become.

She took him by the arm and led him back to the dropship. Soon after, Cameron, Ferrell and the others retreated into the dropship and started the journey back to Camus.

Cameron had survived the impossible and was ready to start a new day. Not just as a slave, but as Ferrell's word and his will. As his enforcer.

"May the gods save me," she said to herself, "welcome to the damned."

SLAVE TRADERS GLOSSARY

Character list

Cameron Lynn Summers: First ascension Telekinetic and Sense-Ranger.
Alex Sheridan: Fifth ascension Ranger Energy-Caster. Enforcer and personal bodyguard to James Ferrell.
James Ferrell: Slave Lord of the Ninth Faction, ruler of Camus and ranking member of the Ninth Faction Council.
Colin Trails: Slave Lord of the old Accaren Empire and wanted criminal of the Human Republic.
Conrad Masters: Slave trader and son of Slave Lord Reid Masters.
Alexandria Morgan: Slave Lord of the old Accaren Empire and leader of the legendary Morgan bounty hunter family.
Aden Stark: Slave Lord of Unexplored-Space.
Damarious Ta'ag: Accaren warrior and bodyguard of Colin Trails.
Saal'li'Mar: Draith Clan Leader. First son of Kar'Raa'desh and Commander of the combined Draith fleet.
No'Vaa: Draith Clan Leader. Fourth son of Kar'Raa'desh and ruler of Cannton.
Rift: Draith Clan Leader. The Seventh son of Kar'Raa'desh, ruler of Salvor and overseer of A'Rend.
Adrian Quin: Member of the Crimson Syndicate and leader of the Ninth Faction Council.
Maglar: Tuskeron of Condor pride. Ruler of Tawson 4 and ranking member of the Ninth Faction Council.
Yen'Ta: Representative of the Turkcanon Consortium and ranking member of the Ninth Faction Council.

Bib'Lek: Representative of the Narairian Hive and member of the Ninth Faction Council.
Captain Logan Masters: Human Republic officer and Wrath squad leader.
Lieutenant Jade Diez: Human officer and second in command to Logan Masters.
Hayden Summers: Fifth ascension Ranger-Technopath and Cameron's last living relative.
Sargus: Rhino-bred Tuskeron. Second in command of security on Camus.
Nora Lyons: James Ferrell's personal slave.

Race overview

Accaren: A-car-ren (double 'C' means K sound, or CK.) Warrior race with no abilities. They use and wear Accaren armor. They are genetically heavier and can handle three times the amount of pain as a Human or Ranger.
A'lur'in: Tall thin aliens with grey skin and black hair. They have advanced reflexes and superior technology. They inhabit Unexplored-Space and are rarely seen in the Known.
A'Zealion: Ah-zeal-ion. Humanoid Shapeshifter. Limited in their ability A'Zealions can transform into animals.
Turkcanon: Tur-cannon (silent K or add K before C) A reptile race with green scales and yellow eyes.
Draith: A hunter race. They stand nearly two and a half meters in height, have advanced reflexes and wear thick armor.
Narairian: Na-rare-ian: Insect race who serves the Queens. Narairians inhabit Known-Space but primarily reside and are from Unexplored-Space.
Ranger: Ability-base Humanoid. Each are born with one if not two ascensions. This could be controlling Fire, advanced reflexes and many others. Each Ranger will have five levels of their ascension. This will give them different abilities throughout their lifetime.

Tuskeron: Tusk-er-on. Animal and Human hybrid. Known Tuskeron breeds. Rhino, Buffalo, and Lion. They are the largest of the Races in Known-Space and have few Human characteristics.
Valari: Va-lari. A spirit or dimensional being. They can inhabit a host through an unknown ritual. They will take on the hosts abilities and will have full access to their memories. This includes Ranger ascensions. They give the host several abilities: Increased speed, advanced healing, and the ability to sense powerful beings. Even if they are planets away.
The Prophets: Ancient Humanoid beings who helped the Rangers hundreds of years before. Current time. No one has seen a Prophet since the Accaren War.
Ninth Faction: An alliance of the lesser powers. Tuskeron Hordes, Turkcanon Consortium, Narairian Hive and the Slave Lords. This alliance has been at odds with the Human Republic since their conception after the Accaren War.
Earth Core Congress or ECC: Human Republic government.

Titles and Events

Slave Lord: A title given to a Human only. Someone who is in control of a region of slavers. (Example: James Ferrell is the Slave Lord of the Ninth Faction.)
Draith Clan Leader: Draith title and is the leader of a clan. This is the highest rank a Draith can be born with and will only answer to Chief Kar'Raa'desh.
Hunt Master: 1. Draith title and is second in command to a Clan Leader. 2. A Draith who has been charged with a solo or group hunt. This is a lifelong title or `hunt'.
Tribe Leader: Accaren title: One who is the leader of an Accaren tribe. (Must be born Accaren and from that tribe to apply)

Accaren War: A long drawn out battle between the Ranger and Accaren Empires. Lasted over fifty years and took place two hundred years prior to the Draith War.

Profanity

Parafek: Para-feck. Origin: Accaren profanity meaning a sex slave or a slave used for sexual purposes. This word has no gender or race tied to it.
Uk': Uck. Origin: Accaren profanity meaning: An Accaren without honor. Slang: A Human beggar covered in shit.
Near'Ti: Origin. Draith profanity meaning `Bastard' or `Seventh son'. (Literally meaning: Unworthy or unwanted offspring)
Stupid Human: Origin: common Ranger insult. Meaning to be Human. To be flawed, incomplete, or preform a task wrong. (Example: The Ranger called him a `stupid Human' for miscounting the Shay-cranes.)
Ranger arrogance: Origin: Human insult meaning to be intitled or sanctimonious. To literally walk with arrogance in every stride. To be controlled by one's emotions.

MAP OF KNOWN-SPACE

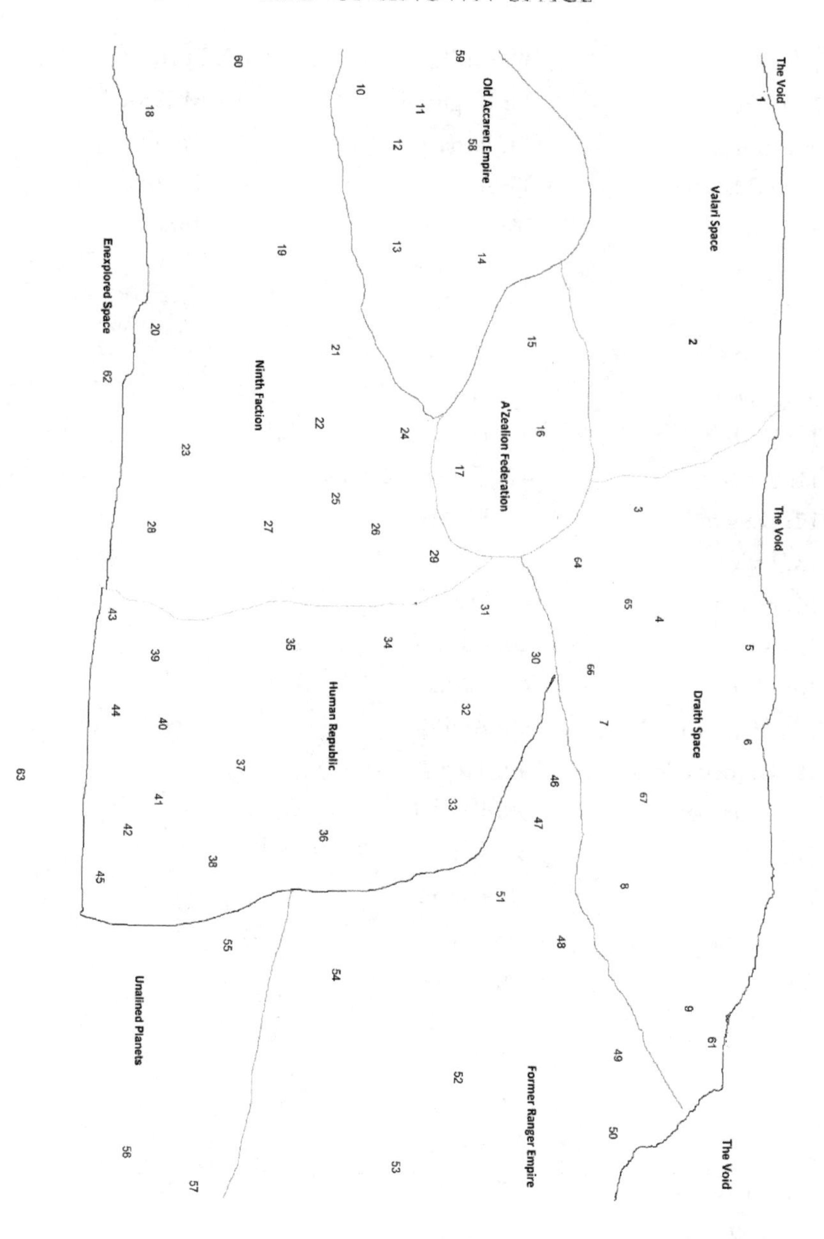

Planet Index

1: Tyris
2: Alitaer
3: Cannton
4: Kar'dan'sia
5: Salvor
6: A'Rend
7: Quia
8: Er'don'ia
9: El'leria
10: Keth
11: Senia
12: Daigys
13: Iceler
14: Kor'ona
15: Ro'ion
16: A'Zeal
17: Cadus-Prime
18: Garocus System
19: Oc'tal'ia
20: Peer
21: Me'er
22: Syprus
23: Camus
24: TS3
25: TS1
26: Korath
27: Vau'Tir
28: Tawson 4
29: TS2
30: Agron
31: Quinn
32: Cal'lia
33: Brighton
34: Jasna
35: Araka
36: Vera 5
37: Ragnar
38: Scion
39: Geniva
40: New Earth
41: Triton
42: Terreth Prisons
43: Kemish
44: Lyari
45: Delayon
46: De'Voy
47: Aathis
48: Aradon
49: Trey
50: Braxton
51: Auctus
52: Rydon
53: Zail
54: Alesia
55: Beshin
56: Renia
57: Corron
58: Loomis
59: Accara
60: Nivar
61: Py'Rath
62: Tenneb
63: Bulvark
64: Miikson
65: Gaa'nor
66: Tatith
67: Bor'rel

CPSIA information can be obtained
at www.ICGtesting.com
Printed in the USA
LVHW010845100721
692198LV00011B/611